# Philadelphia: Street Justice

# Philadelphia: Street Justice

Treasure Hernandez

*www.urbanbooks.net*

Urban Books, LLC
78 East Industry Court
Deer Park, NY 11729

ISBN 13: 978-1-60162-551-9
ISBN 10: 1-60162-551-0

First Printing June 2013
Printed in the United States of America

10 9 8 7 6 5 4 3 2 1

*This is a work of fiction. Any references or similarities to
actual events, real people, living or dead, or to real locales
are intended to give the novel a sense of reality. Any simi-
larity in other names, characters, places, and incidents is
entirely coincidental.*

Distributed by Kensington Publishing Corp.
Submit Wholesale Orders to:
Kensington Publishing Corp.
C/O Penguin Group (USA) Inc.
Attention: Order Processing
405 Murray Hill Parkway
East Rutherford, NJ 07073-2316
Phone: 1-800-526-0275
Fax: 1-800-227-9604

# Prologue

"Don't go. Stay home tonight," Billie pleaded with her father. She stood in front of the living room window where she had just been watching the snow falling, violently swirling in the whipping winds.

"I have to, baby." Her father, Reggie, chuckled a little at his only child's passionate plea. She looked so cute standing there that he couldn't help himself.

"Daddy, please. It's Christmas Eve. Santa is coming." She pouted. "Plus it's bedtime." She gestured to her holiday-themed pajamas. Like every child who believes in Santa Claus, Billie had put her pajamas on and gotten ready for bed several hours early.

"I have to work. The buses don't stop running because it's Christmas Eve." He scooped eight-year-old Billie into his arms. She sat in the crook of his arm with her legs wrapped around his waist and her arms around his neck.

Reggie had been a city bus driver on the same route in Philadelphia for fifteen years. He wasn't scheduled to work this night, but one of the other drivers had called in sick, so he volunteered to drive. He was always willing to work for extra pay. He and his wife, Monique, were saving up to move out of North Philly and buy a house in the suburbs.

"It's snowing too much." She squeezed him tight. Billie was going to think of every argument she could to keep her father from going out. She never liked when her father went off to work, especially if it was Christmas. She desperately wanted him to stay in.

"I'll make sure to drive extra careful. And I'll tell you what—if I see Santa, I'll tell him to be extra generous this year."

"No, Daddy. If you're awake, Santa won't come in and leave presents."

"Oh, right." Reggie acted like he had forgotten this important detail. "I'll make sure to be home and in bed before Santa comes. But in case he comes early while I'm still working, you should get to sleep now." He hugged his daughter and kissed her cheek. They shared their high cheekbones, and when either of them smiled, their faces filled out into a joyful look.

She smiled. "Okay, Daddy." Billie slid out of her father's grasp, and watched him kiss his wife then walk out the door into the cold, stormy night.

The streets were deserted as Reggie drove to the bus depot. The combination of the holiday and the storm chased all of Philadelphia into their homes. Reggie didn't mind it; in fact, he liked it. He had grown up in the city and was ready to get out. He wanted to move to the quiet, tree-lined streets of the suburbs.

Reggie daydreamed about his future as he carefully maneuvered his car through the empty streets. He was ready and excited for the move, especially now that his dream was in sight. In a little more than a month, they would have saved enough for a down payment. Thinking about all the years he and Monique struggled to put money into savings, he smiled at the thought that they were finally close to their goal. He loved his family and would do anything for them.

The bus depot was just as deserted as the city. Bus service was cut back on a holiday schedule, so many of the drivers had the night off.

"What's up, Reggie? Gonna be a quiet night tonight." DeShawn, the dispatcher, greeted Reggie with a nod.

"Yeah, not many people out there." Reggie opened his locker. "Just let me get through this shift and get home. I got me some Christmas to start celebrating."

"I hear that. Don't even know why you would be coming in tonight anyway."

"Get me some overtime. Almost got enough for a house. Time to get the fuck out the ghetto."

"Well, you lucky that motherfucker Jerry don't like working and always be looking for someone to run his shift."

"I'll take the extra cash. That stupid son of a bitch always complaining about being broke, but never wants to work." Reggie shook his head in disgust and closed his locker.

"Yeah, he a fool. Bus 624 is ready. Got the chains on the tires." Deshawn handed Reggie a clipboard so he could sign in for the bus.

Reggie handed the clipboard back. "A'ight, son. See you after my shift."

"Nah. I'm done in a few hours. My ass'll be long gone, relaxing and starting my holiday."

"I hear that." They laughed and pounded fists.

As Reggie drove his route, he thought more about moving his family out of the hard city streets to somewhere beautiful. More than anything, he wanted to give that to his baby girl. He daydreamed for the next few hours, until a little past midnight, when the weather started getting even worse. Reggie now turned his full attention to his driving.

The wind and snow were still pounding the city and showed no signs of stopping. In fact, it might have been a pretty sight if he were watching it through the window with his daughter. For most of the shift, the bus had been empty. There had been only a handful of passengers all night. It seemed the only other people on the roads were the ones driving the snowplows, and they were having a hard time keeping the streets clear.

As Reggie drove down the street, he got a call from dispatch telling him that bus service was being cancelled. All he needed to do was make it to the end of the route, turn the bus around, and take it back to the depot. The Christmas holiday was about to begin for Reggie, and he couldn't have been happier.

"Aw, shit! Half a shift and full holiday pay. A Christmas miracle." Reggie's voice echoed through the empty bus.

Reggie made the turn at the end of the route and headed for the depot. Through the swiping windshields and snow, he could see a young man with his hood pulled over his head standing at the first bus stop. As the bus got closer, the young man started waving his arms to signal the bus to stop. Reggie carefully pulled into the stop and opened the door.

"Hop on," Reggie said.

The passenger stepped on the bus and paid the fare without speaking to Reggie.

"You're lucky. They just suspended bus service. I'm heading back in, but I'm feeling generous, so I'll give you a ride." Reggie closed the bus door.

The young man sat in the first seat. He kept his hood on and remained silent.

Reggie made small talk with his new passenger. "It's nasty out there tonight. At least we know it's gonna be a white Christmas."

"Yep," the passenger mumbled.

Reggie glanced over at his passenger, who was sitting with his hands stuffed in his pockets. He couldn't have been more than fifteen years old.

"What you doin' out so late? Shouldn't you be in waiting to open presents tomorrow morning?"

"Fuck that. You need to shut the fuck up." The young man pulled a gun from his coat pocket and pointed it at Reggie.

"Whoa, young buck. Calm down. I ain't got no money for you."

"Kareem says you late with his payment. You gotta pay, muthafucka."

"I don't know what you talkin' about. Who's Kareem?"

"Fuck you, old man. You know damn well what I'm talkin' 'bout. Now, either you give me Kareem's money or you gonna pay another way."

"Now hold on. I'm tellin' you, I don't know no Kareem." By this time, Reggie had pulled the bus over to the side of the road.

The young man stood up and moved toward Reggie. "Give me the fuckin' money, Jerry." He punched Reggie in the side of his head.

The blow was so sudden that Reggie saw stars, and his head rang. He muffled a reflexive cry, and tasted the iron of blood; he must have bitten his tongue. He tried to shake it off, and said, "Hold on. I'm not Jerry. You got the wrong guy."

The young man cut him off, and said with pride, "Don't bullshit me. I know this your bus route, nigga." He'd done his homework. Jerry wasn't going to fool him with some lame-ass nonsense like that. No one was going to fool him.

"I'm just filling in. Jerry called out tonight. This ain't my normal route."

At this, the kid hesitated. He hadn't expected an excuse like that.

Reggie could sense that he'd taken the young man off-guard, so he continued to try talking him down. "Jerry's always calling out, man. I'm just trying to get some extra work, give my little girl a merry Christmas, you know?"

For a minute Reggie thought he was getting through to him, but then the young man shook his head violently. "Nah, fuck you." The young man punched Reggie again.

"Okay, okay," yelled Reggie, putting his hands up. He realized he wasn't going to be able to reason with this young man. He could see the nervousness in the kid's face and he sensed that this situation wasn't going to end by talking.

"Let me get my money from my pocket." He looked at the kid and waited for his answer. The boy stepped back to let Reggie stand up.

As soon as Reggie was out of his seat, he lunged at the boy and tried to grab the gun from his hands. They struggled for control of the gun. The kid was stronger than Reggie expected. The boy started getting the upper hand, and when he had the chance, he fired a shot into Reggie's chest.

"Fuck you, Jerry." The boy seethed as Reggie fell in the aisle.

Reggie struggled to speak. "I'm not Jerry. Call an ambulance." The bullet had lodged in his left lung, and the blood was flowing freely from the hole it had made in his chest.

The boy rummaged through Reggie's pockets and found his wallet. He took the money from its folds, and was about to throw everything else on the ground when he noticed Reggie's ID.

"Oh, fuck," the boy said, panicked. "Oh, fuck, man." He covered his face, gun still in hand, and swore at himself for making the mistake, swore at this punk for getting in his way, and swore at Jerry for not being where he was supposed to be.

When the dispatch radio crackled to life, reminding him where he was, he pulled himself together quick. Instead of throwing the wallet on the ground, he stuffed it into his coat pocket. He pointed the gun at Reggie and pumped two bullets into his forehead, eliminating any chance of Reggie being able to identify his attacker.

Then, without looking back, the boy stepped over the dead body, and ran off into the stormy night.


It was a Christmas Billie would never forget. She came running into the living room ready to rip open presents and was stopped by her mother, who was waiting for her.

"Billie, sit down dear," her mother said.

Billie saw a look on her mother's face that she had never seen before. The uneasiness, this look caused Billie, upset her. Billie sensed something wrong.

"What, Mama?" Billie sat where her mother directed her. Her eyes were wide and her chin was beginning to tremble slightly from nervousness.

Billie sat and waited for her mother to speak. Her mother didn't say anything; she just sat and stared at Billie with a sad look on her face. She took Billie's hands in hers and began gently rubbing them.

Billie broke the silence. "Mama?"

"Billie, I have something to tell you. It's about your father." Her mother paused as her eyes started to tear up.

"What about Daddy?" Billie was scared.

"Your daddy is not coming home." The tears started falling from her eyes.

"Why not? He has to be here to open presents." Tears began to fall from Billie's eyes as well. At this point the tears were more a reaction to the way her mother was acting than anything else.

There was no easy way for her mother to say it so she came right out with it. "Your father died last night."

Billie stared blankly at her mother as the stream of tears became heavier. Billie didn't know what to say or what to do. She was scared, confused, sad, angry, nervous, guilty, stressed. She was a ball of emotions and didn't know which one she felt the most.

When she finally spoke all she could muster in a soft whisper was, "Why?"

Her mother began stroking Billie's hair. "I don't know, baby. God has a plan and needed him, I guess."

"But I need Daddy," Billie said.

"I know, baby, I know. Me too." She kissed Billie on her forehead.

"It's not fair." Billie got up from the chair and went back to her room. She was devastated. She spent the rest of the day crying in her room. The presents stayed under the tree, untouched, forgotten.

She came out of the room only a few times over the next two days. Late at night on the second day of her grieving, Billie walked into the kitchen to get some food. There was a newspaper on the kitchen table with a picture of her father on the front page. Billie started reading the accompanying article. Billie didn't understand a lot of it but she did understand that a bad man had shot her daddy. The article said something about how the bus was driving through a section of town that was run by a man named Kareem, who was a drug dealer. It said the police had asked Kareem questions but he told them about something called an alibi. Billie wanted to know why the police hadn't found the man who shot her daddy.

After reading the article something shifted inside of Billie. She no longer felt scared or confused. She wanted the man responsible for killing her daddy to pay a price. She wanted to make sure that men who did bad things were punished. At that moment Billie stopped crying for her daddy. She had done enough crying alone in her room. She told herself that she needed to be strong for her mama.

Four days after Christmas, Billie stood with her head held high as they lowered her daddy's casket into the ground. As she watched the casket come to rest in the ground she turned to her mother and said, "Mommy, I promise I'm going to make someone pay for this."

# Chapter 1

Twenty years later . . .

"Guilty." The judge slammed the gavel down.

Billie Powell's star was steadily rising as an assistant district attorney, and this victory was another step up the ladder.

She stood and watched as the perp was handcuffed and escorted out of the courtroom. Billie's face showed no emotion. It never did in the courtroom. The minute she started a case she was all business. She took every case personally, and her drive and determination were earning her a reputation as a "pit bull" attorney. When other lawyers saw they were going up against Billie Powell, they knew it was going to be a nasty fight. She was determined to prosecute every criminal to the fullest extent, and she almost never offered a plea deal to the accused criminals. The few times she had, she was a young attorney just starting out, and even then it was only because of pressure from her bosses. If it had been up to her, no one would ever get a deal. As time went on and Billie established herself in the office, her bosses were starting to give her more leeway. As long as she was winning, they stayed out of her way.

The courtroom was full of action. The observers were all talking to each other, giving their opinions about the verdict; the judge was clearing his desk; and the reporters were all talking into their voice recorders, replaying the events of the trial for the award-winning stories they were planning to write. Billie remained silent as she packed her briefcase and walked out of the courtroom.

Kevin, one of her colleagues, called out to her, "Come have a beer with us."

"I think I'll pass," Billie responded.

He made his pitch. "Come on. Celebrate our win. You never come out with us."

Billie had always sensed that Kevin was attracted to her. He was a nice enough guy and good at his job, but Billie didn't want to date anyone in her office. It was a rule she had for herself. Her life was complicated enough without the drama of fucking someone she worked with every day. Not to mention she just wasn't that into white guys.

"I'm good. Maybe next time. I've got some business to take care of."

Kevin shook his head as he looked at Billie's perfect body in her charcoal gray Prada pencil skirt with matching suit jacket. She dressed like a true professional but had the body of a video vixen. "You've always got an excuse. You need to not work so much. Enjoy yourself every now and then."

"Thanks for the advice. I'll be sure to tell the families affected by crime that I can't work on their case because you said I need to enjoy myself." Billie walked away.

Kevin had nothing to say in response as he watched her leave the building. He felt sorry for Billie because she couldn't relax for even one afternoon.

Even though she had just won another case she wasn't satisfied. No matter how much time a criminal got she always thought they deserved more. This case was no different. If Billie had her way every criminal she prosecuted would get a life sentence. Billie wanted to go scorched-earth on the entire criminal world.

Billie headed straight back to her office. There was more work to be done, more criminals to punish. There was always someone else who needed to pay for crimes committed.

She flung her briefcase onto her desk with more force than needed and flopped down into her chair. What was her next move? What would satisfy her? She stared at her blank computer screen. She thought about how empty she felt after all of her cases lately. The excitement she would feel after a win when she first started out was gone. Slowly over time that energy began to disappear. She had started out her law career for one purpose: to punish as many criminals as she could. It was Billie's way of honoring her father. After every win she knew that she was making a difference. Now she wasn't so sure she was making a difference. She needed more; she needed something else to give her that satisfaction she used to get when she used the law to punish a criminal. After a few moments, she turned on the computer to begin searching for the one thing that would satisfy her.

"Here you are. You'll do nicely," she said to herself after a half hour of reading files. She clicked the print button. She snatched the paper from the printer, eased back in her chair, and reread the file.

"Why aren't you out celebrating another victory, Powell?"

Billie jumped a little in her seat. Stanley Lewis, the district attorney, had materialized in her doorway from out of nowhere. Billie swore sometimes that this guy was a ghost.

"No reason to celebrate, sir." As she responded to him, she discreetly reached for her mouse and closed the file on her computer.

"Nonsense. You should always celebrate a victory."

"These drug dealers, thieves, and murderers deserve worse than a few years behind bars."

"Well, I agree, but the laws say we can only do so much."

"And I prosecute them to the max, but it still isn't satisfying to know that they will most likely be released at some point."

"You can't dwell on that." The DA changed the subject. "Anyway, nice job, Powell. You keep racking up these wins and you'll be in line for my job. I better watch my back." He smiled wickedly.

"I don't think you have to worry about that, sir," Billie replied politely, but she was thinking, *You damn right I should have your job.* Even though personally they never had any problems, Billie thought that Stanley Lewis was too soft on criminals. She always thought if she had his position she would start cracking the whip and demanding more from the ADAs.

"Go home, Powell. You deserve the rest of the day off."

"You're right. I think I will take some personal time." Billie pushed her chair back from her desk.

"Good." DA Lewis winked and walked away.

Billie couldn't figure her boss out. He was definitely happy that she kept winning her cases, but she felt that maybe he really was getting nervous she would take his job. Billie figured that his job was important to him because he spent so much time rubbing shoulders with politicians to get in their good graces. She always saw him kissing up to someone in the city government. Billie wouldn't put it past him to be paranoid that someone would be gunning for his job. Although she never had to be careful before, she made a mental note to keep her guard up with her boss. Billie's motto: never trust people with two first names.

She stuffed the single sheet of paper into her briefcase, shut down her computer, and was out the door.

While driving home, she began planning out her evening. The more she thought about it, the more she became filled with excitement and anticipation: the same feelings she would get the night before she knew she was going to win a case.

She was planning on a late night and probably wouldn't be eating later, so when she got home, she cooked herself a quick bite to eat. As she sat at her kitchen table eating her meal, she studied the paper she had printed from her computer. Billie had a wicked grin on her face as she read the file.

"Time to party." She wiped her mouth, rose from the table, and put the dishes in the dishwasher.

Billie showered and got fresh for her night out. She applied more makeup than she usually wore. Some heavy purple eye shadow with extra eyeliner complemented the dark cherry lipstick on her succulent lips. The blush she applied accented her high cheekbones to perfection.

She opened her closet and flipped through the hanging clothes. She found a nice, slightly sheer black top so that in the right light you could see she wore no bra. She matched the top with some skin-tight Gucci jeans. The Louboutin heels she wore elongated her muscular legs.

She stood in front of her full-length mirror and admired herself. Along with her long, muscular legs, she was stacked in all the right places—booty that wouldn't quit, small waist, and nice, firm breasts.

It excited Billie to get dressed in her "going out" clothes. When she changed into these clothes, she was a different person. It meant that she was going out to blow off some steam and satisfy her needs.

Happy with her outfit choice, Billie jumped in her car and drove from her West Oak Lane neighborhood to the Fairhill section of Philadelphia. She parked her car on North Front Street and pulled out the paper she had printed earlier. Billie double-checked the address, picture, and name of the man she was about to meet.

"It's on." She was ready for action.

Billie got out of her car and walked down the block. North Front Street was dark and deserted. The lone streetlight on the block had been shot out, and the little sliver of moon was not illuminating anything. She passed a beauty salon, two Spanish restaurants, a Laundromat, and an auto supply store. All of their smells blended together: the chemicals of the beauty salon, the spicy Spanish food, laundry detergent, and car oil. All had their iron gates pulled down to keep the thieves out for the night. She was disgusted that honest business owners had to fear their own neighborhood. As anxious as she was about being here, she almost dared the city to put her face to face with a scumbag who might feel like breaking into one of these establishments.

Billie stopped in front of the dilapidated two-story building and took a deep breath to calm herself. She walked up the three small, broken concrete steps to the front door and knocked. There was some rustling on the other side of the door, and her heart began to speed up with anticipation.

The door opened slightly; the chain lock stopped it from opening wider.

"Hello?" a man said through the small opening.

"Hey, I'm Crystal. Your man sent me over. Said you just been released and needed a good time."

Billie watched through the crack in the door as the man looked to her left and right then behind her. Convinced that no one was waiting to jump him, he finally took the time to check out the fine woman standing at his door.

Billie could see the smile spread on the man's face.

"Hell yeah," he said. He closed the door and unlatched the chain to let Billie in.

Billie stepped through the door and entered a mostly empty living room. To Billie's right there was one recliner with a TV tray next to it. Sitting in front of that was a small television atop a milk crate, and that was it; no more furniture, nothing on the walls except a layer of dirt. She focused on the recliner. It was vinyl, with rips and tears revealing whatever stuffing was left inside. Her father used to have a recliner, she remembered. They would cuddle there together sometimes in its warm fabric.

"I like what you've done with the place," Billie said sarcastically.

"The fuck you expect, bitch? I just got out the pen two days ago." The man snarled with irritation.

She turned to him. "I know, baby. I'm just playin'." She stroked his cheek softly. This calmed him down immediately.

She continued, "You're Ramon, right?"

"Yeah, baby. That's right."

"Well, Ramon, since there is no place to sit in this room, why don't you show me to the bedroom."

"I like the way you thinkin', girl." He led her toward the back of the house. "Yo, who you say sent you? Phareed?"

"Don't worry about who sent me. Just know you've earned my visit."

"Hell yeah, it's Phareed. That nigga is payin' me back for not snitchin'. You know I had to dead a nigga for Phareed? Well, I deaded more than that, but I only got caught for one. I coulda snitched that nigga out and saved my ass, but I ain't like that. I'm a loyal nigga. Did a fifteen-year bid off that shit—well, I only did seven of those fifteen."

"Don't worry, honey. I know all about you," Billie purred.

Ramon smiled. "Yeah, I'm pro'ly kinda famous up in the hood."

"Something like that."

The bedroom was just as barren as the living room. The only thing in the room was a dirty-ass twin bed and a nightstand with an alarm clock sitting on it.

"I know my place don't look nice now, but I'ma get back on my feet. I'ma call Phareed, tell him it's time start working for him again. Yo, believe me, you work for him, you make mad duckets."

"Don't you worry 'bout all that right now. You just need to make sure this kitty is going to purr." She seductively slid her hand between her thighs.

"I'm gonna tear that shit up."

"Then sit down and let this bitch do her thang." She pushed Ramon softly in the chest, guiding him back toward the bed.

He plopped down on the edge of the bed and quickly started unbuckling his belt. Billie got on her knees, set her purse on the floor next to her, and helped Ramon out of his pants. She pulled his jeans down to his knees, exposing his erect, thick penis.

"Mmmm. You got more than enough for me to break off a little somethin'. Lie back, daddy." Again, she softly pushed his chest. He obeyed. She grabbed hold of his dick with her left hand and began to stroke it slowly. With her right hand she reached into her purse.

Ramon heard her open the purse and looked up from his prone position. "What you doing?"

"I'm looking for a condom, daddy. Lie back and close those eyes."

Again, Ramon obeyed. He liked the way this bitch was taking charge. He hadn't fucked a woman or gotten his dick sucked in a minute, and he wasn't about to fuck that shit up. First some head, and then he was planning on tearing that pussy to pieces.

"Do your thang, girl." He closed his eyes.

Billie found what she was looking for. With her left hand she grabbed on to the head of Ramon's dick; with her right she grabbed a pair of pruning shears. With one swift motion, she pulled the shears from her purse and cut Ramon's dick off at the base.

Ramon immediately shot up, and as he did, Billie plunged the shears up and into the underside of his chin. The tip of the shears tore through the skin and into his mouth, puncturing Ramon's tongue.

Billie jumped up from her knees to avoid the blood that was now spewing from Ramon's groin and neck. She dropped his penis, grabbed her purse, pulled out a hunting knife, and slit Ramon's throat.

He was rendered silent. He struggled to try to stop the bleeding from his neck with one hand as he pulled the shears from his chin with the other. His attempts were useless. After a few moments of struggling, he went into shock and passed out from the loss of blood.

Billie took out some baby wipes from her purse, picked up Ramon's penis, washed off any trace of fingerprints, and then did the same with the pruning shears.

"Unlucky for you, you only did seven years. If you did fifteen, I wouldn't have found you today in the files of released criminals. There's your payback for past crimes, motherfucker." Billie calmly walked out of the house and back to her car a satisfied woman.

When Billie promised her mother that someone would pay for her father's death, this was what she meant. It just took her twenty years to realize it.

# Chapter 2

Detective Walter Peterson stood over the bloody body with his notepad in hand. "Jesus. They chopped his dick off. That's some coldhearted shit." He scribbled a few notes. "We need to find out if this guy had any girlfriends, or who his exes are," he said to his new partner, D'Angelo Martin.

"Maybe one who works at a flower shop." D'Angelo nodded to the pruning shears on the bed.

"Did we dust for prints on these?" Walter asked the forensics guy.

"Yeah, came back clean," he answered.

"Figures."

"You know this is the third guy in the last two months who's been released then murdered," D'Angelo said to Walter.

"I was thinking the same thing. We need to start looking at the similarities between them," Walter answered.

Walter liked his new partner. He was skeptical at first because the kid had just been promoted to detective, but Walter had to remind himself that he was once in the same position as D'Angelo. When Walter got promoted to detective, he was paired with Detective Jerrod Jefferson.

*Jerrod was a veteran of the force and didn't like having to work with anyone. Needless to say, when he was paired with a rookie, he wasn't too happy. Jerrod made life for Walter as difficult as he could and made him prove himself every step of the way. Walter hated Jerrod at first and almost requested a transfer, but his pride won out and he vowed to show his mentor that he was a damn good detective.*

*"Why don't you let me do anything, Jefferson?" a young Walter asked his partner and mentor as they headed to the crime scene.*

*"'Cause you don't know shit." Jerrod kept his eyes on the road as he drove.*

*"Then teach me," Walter answered*

*"Just keep your head down and your mouth shut."*

*"How the fuck am I going to learn anything by doing that?"*

*"Watch your tongue, boy," Jerrod warned.*

*"I'm not watching shit. I'm sick of your grumpy ass treating me like dirt. You need to start letting me work these cases."*

*"I'm warning you, boy."*

*"I ain't your boy. I'm warning you. Stop calling me that shit."*

*"Or what?" Jerrod chuckled.*

*"I'll fuck you up."*

*Jerrod pulled the car over immediately. "I'd like to see you try." He stepped out of the car and on to the busy sidewalk. Walter did the same.*

*As soon as Walter stepped on the sidewalk, Jerrod sucker-punched him. Walter's instincts took over. He swung right back and hit Jerrod in the mouth. The fight was on. The two men traded blows and wrestled as a crowd gathered around them. People were watching and cheering like they were at an MMA fight. Neither man would surrender, and the fight continued until a police cruiser pulled up. At the sound of the siren, the men broke apart, although they still eyed each other like they were ready to pounce again at any moment.*

*The men both pulled out their badges as the officers approached.*

*"Detectives," one of the officers greeted them uncertainly. The officers were not expecting two detectives to be fighting each other. They hesitated, not really knowing how to approach the situation.*

*"What's going on?" the other officer asked.*

*"Just a misunderstanding. We're good now," Jerrod answered.*

*"Yeah, we're good," Walter said.*

*"Okay, Detectives, if you say so." The first officer turned to the crowd. "All right, nothing more to see. Keep it moving."*

Walter and Jerrod had gotten back in the car bloody and bruised. From that point on, Jerrod changed his attitude toward the rookie detective. Walter had stepped up and shown that he was a man and Jerrod respected that. Their relationship became strong, and they stayed partners until Jerrod retired last month.

Now Walter was the veteran mentoring the rookie. His approach was going to be different than his old partner's. There would be no fighting with his partner to prove his manhood. Walter was going to make sure this partnership started off much smoother.

"Any cameras in the area?" Walter asked one of the officers on the scene. "That might give us a look at who did this."

"No, sir. Checked with all the businesses. No one has security cameras."

"Anyone see anything?" Walter asked.

"We're in the process of interviewing neighbors. Nothing yet."

Walter flipped through his notepad, hoping that a magic answer might appear. "You got anything?" he asked D'Angelo.

"I could almost guarantee this guy is connected to the other two."

Walter nodded in agreement. "Get back to us after you finish up the interviews."

"Will do, Detective," the officer responded.

D'Angelo handed the officer his card.

"All right, let's get back to the station and start putting these pieces together," Walter said.

"Let's do it." D'Angelo followed Walter out of the house.

There was a crowd gathered around the police tape roping off the entrance to the house. Walter saw officers questioning people in the crowd, but he wasn't hopeful that anyone would give them information. There was a code in the hood that was rarely broken: even if you know something, don't tell the police shit.

Walter ducked under the tape and held it for D'Angelo as the crowd moved out of their way.

"Yo, what happened?" one of the girls from the beauty salon asked.

"You tell me," Walter answered and kept walking to the car.

"So we got three bodies, all released from lockup, and within days they are murdered. Seems like too much of a coincidence. What's the connection?" D'Angelo said as Walter drove them back to the station.

"They're all grimy-ass dudes." Both men chuckled at Walter's little joke.

Walter pulled the car into their parking space in front of the station. D'Angelo's cell phone rang.

"Detective Martin," he answered the call.

Walter could hear a male voice on the other end of the phone, but couldn't make out what he was saying.

"Hold on, Officer Greene." D'Angelo pulled out his notepad and raised his eyebrows at Walter. "Okay, go on."

D'Angelo jotted down notes as Officer Greene spoke. When the officer finished, D'Angelo said, "Great work, Greene. If we need anything else, I'll get back to you." D'Angelo hung up the phone.

He turned to his partner and said, "We got a partial description of a woman who was seen leaving the victim's house last night." D'Angelo's voice was laced with optimism.

"Let me see." Walter took the notepad from D'Angelo and read the description.

When he was finished, he handed the notepad back to D'Angelo. "I'll meet you inside."

"Okay. This is good, right?" D'Angelo was surprised that his partner didn't seem more excited about the potential break in the case.

Walter simply nodded.

As soon as D'Angelo stepped out of the car and shut the door, Walter took out his cell phone and made a call.

# Chapter 3

Billie walked into her office with a bounce to her step. She was always in a good mood the morning after a kill. She sat down at her desk with a big smile on her face, ready to start a new case and put someone behind bars. Her energy level was high considering she'd barely slept the night before.

After she left Ramon's house Billie couldn't calm down. She was so high with adrenaline she contemplated finding a corner boy and slicing his throat, but after some thought, she decided to go straight home instead. She wasn't about to chance getting pulled over by the police and questioned about why she was out so late or why she had blood on her clothes.

As she was lying in bed thinking about her latest kill, she found her hand sliding between her legs. Her vagina was already wet as her fingers started to slowly rub her clit. She spread her lips and plunged two fingers deep inside and gave herself a nice finger fucking. Her rhythm started slow and sped up as she became more and more turned on. It didn't take long for her to have a monster orgasm.

In her post-orgasm haze, she told herself that it wasn't the killing that she enjoyed, but the justice that she was serving. She was ridding the world of evil and keeping her city safe. She was a public servant doing bad to do good. She needed to do this because it frightened her that she was enjoying killing so much. She was struggling with the fact that she might be becoming one of the same people she was so hell-bent on punishing. She made sure to remind herself that it was all for the good of society.

Thinking about the previous night got Billie so excited she couldn't sit at her desk any longer. She walked down the hall to the office pantry to get some hot herbal tea.

"Hey, Billie." Kevin walked up behind her as she was steeping the tea bag.

"Shit!" His sudden appearance startled Billie, causing her to spill a little of her tea.

"Oh, sorry. I didn't mean to scare you." Kevin grabbed some napkins and handed one to Billie.

"No worries. It's my fault." Billie smiled as she and Kevin wiped the counter dry.

"You're in a better mood than yesterday," Kevin said.

"I had a good night." Billie smirked and threw the wet napkin in the trash.

"You spend it with that boring-ass cop?" Kevin rolled his eyes.

"For your information, he is a detective, and what I did is none of your business."

"Well, whatever you did, it put you in a better mood than winning our case did."

"How can I be happy after winning a case when I know that in a few years whoever I put behind bars will probably be back on the streets?"

"You're bringing justice and punishing them for their crimes."

"In my opinion, they never get punished enough when lawyers get involved." Billie frowned. This was an argument she and Kevin had after almost every case. She couldn't understand why he was so satisfied when those scumbags always got much less than what they deserved from a weak judicial system.

"If I won as many cases as you did, I'd be happy." Kevin shrugged his shoulders. "Hey, you hear about that homicide over in Fairhill? Guy got his dick chopped off."

Billie smiled. "He must have deserved it." She sipped her tea. "Nice talking with you, Kevin." She walked back to her office, proud of the work she had done the previous night and the fact that it had already hit the newswire. She couldn't wait to get back to her desk and read the online articles about the murder. She was definitely making a statement with this latest kill.

Billie's phone was ringing as she entered her office.

"This is Billie," she answered as set her mug on her desk.

"Where were you last night?"

"Good morning to you too, Walter." Billie and Walter had been casually hooking up for six months.

"Good morning, Billie. Now, where were you last night?" Walter asked.

"I was home."

"I called you. Why didn't you answer?"

"I saw your messages. I was just about to call you. I was so wiped out from my case yesterday. I went straight home, shut off my phones, and went to sleep." Billie wished she had a better excuse, but it was the best she could do in the moment. She had seen Walter's call come in but let it go to voice mail. She'd had a more important date with Ramon to attend to. Besides, Walter wasn't her boyfriend; he was just a guy she liked hanging out with. She didn't owe him anything.

"We were supposed to have dinner last night." Some anger was evident in Walter's voice.

"I forgot." Billie matched the anger in Walter's voice with some of her own.

"You forgot? You really know how to make a guy feel special."

"Look, I'm only human. I had a case on my mind, I fell asleep; I forgot. Don't take it so personally."

"You'd rather have your case rock you to sleep than me. How am I not supposed to take something like that personally?"

She huffed out a sigh. "How many times do I have to tell you? Work comes first."

"We need to talk."

"So talk," Billie said.

"Not on the phone. In person."

"Lunch?" Billie suggested.

"No. Tonight. My place."

"All right. Tonight," Billie agreed.

"Don't forget, Billie." Walter hung up.

Billie was surprised by Walter's reaction. He was usually calm and would jump at the chance to have lunch with her. Something was different.

# Chapter 4

Billie pulled into the driveway of Walter's house located in Lower Merion Township. She looked at the two-story house with its manicured lawn and took a deep breath. Billie didn't like the quiet suburb where Walter lived; she liked living in the city and the action the urban environment provided. She was born and bred a city girl and never wanted to leave. Her parents may have wanted to leave but that was never Billie's desire. She was a Philly girl through and through.

Her earlier conversation with Walter had been on her mind all day and was giving her a bad feeling in her gut. She kept going over her movements from the night before to make sure she didn't miss anything. What if Walter had shown up to her house and seen that she wasn't really home? He had never popped by unannounced before but there's always a first time for everything. What would she tell him? Did she leave something at the crime scene to incriminate herself? *Not possible,* she decided. She was too cautious for that.

"Fuck it. Here we go," she said to herself.

Walter answered the door with his pit bull, Apollo, standing by his side. He had bought the dog when he moved into his house to protect it during the day. Billie liked the dog but thought that Walter was ridiculous for thinking he needed protection in this sleepy-ass town.

"Come in." Billie couldn't read Walter's expressionless face as he stepped to the side to let her in.

Billie walked straight to the living room and waited for Walter to take the lead. There was an odd tension between the two that hadn't been there before. Billie didn't know if she should sit or stand or what. Before she knew where he was coming from and what this was about, she was going to stay cool. *Get the information you need before you make any moves.* That was her play in this situation.

"You want something to drink?" Walter asked.

"I'm good." Billie sat on the couch. Normally she would tuck her feet up under her when she sat on this couch, but tonight felt more formal than before, so she kept her feet on the floor.

Walter left Billie in the living room as he went to the kitchen and cracked open a beer. He reentered the living room, sat across from Billie, and took a swig of his beer before setting it down on the side table. He didn't say anything. He just looked at Billie with that blank look that she couldn't read.

Billie was getting annoyed at this little show. She wasn't some hoodlum in an interrogation room who Walter was trying to play. She was the bitch he was fucking. *So get on with it. Show some respect.* She was about ready to scream, "Just tell me what you want, motherfucker! Stop this little act of yours."

"Well?" Billie frowned.

"Well, what?" he answered.

"You said you wanted to talk, so talk."

He nodded. "All right. What's going on? I feel like you haven't been honest with me."

"I told you I turned my phones off last night. I was in bed and asleep by nine o'clock." Billie became defensive, even though she was lying.

"I'm not talking about last night. I mean you seem to be holding something back and pulling away lately."

Billie was relieved to know this had nothing to do with the murder she had committed. He was right that she had been holding something back; it just had nothing to do with their relationship.

"What are you talking about? I'm here, aren't I?" she said, a little snippy.

"Billie—" He stopped himself to gather his thoughts. He wanted to make sure he was saying exactly what he wanted to say. He clenched his jaw and took a few deep breaths.

"What?" Billie was impatient.

"I want more, okay? I want more from you, from us. I want to spend more time with you. I want to know that I am the only man in your life, because you are the only woman I want in mine." The words rushed out of him like compressed air being released from a soda bottle.

Billie said nothing for a second as she absorbed what Walter had just said. She needed to answer this very carefully. There was no way in hell she could give him more right now, but she didn't want to give him up either.

"I barely have time for you. How could I have any time for another guy?" Billie answered.

"Maybe that's why you don't have time for me, because you are spending it with other dudes."

"Don't be ridiculous. All I do is work and occasionally hang out with you." Billie dismissed his theory by swiping her hand in the air like she was shooing a fly.

"Hang out with me more."

"I can't. Not right now. My work is my main priority."

"Stop being so obsessed with work. You can't put every criminal behind bars."

"I can damn well try." Billie was emphatic.

Her forcefulness halted the conversation. It was becoming heated, and neither wanted to get into an argument. There was genuine affection and admiration between the two; they just needed different things from each other. Billie needed space, and Walter needed more commitment.

After a few moments of silence that allowed for both to calm down, Billie spoke. "I'm giving you all that I can right now. My life is complicated. I don't want you mixed up with it. Just give me some time and I promise to give you more later." Billie wasn't certain she would be able to give him more later but she wasn't ready yet to let go of Walter completely.

Walter moved to sit next to Billie on the couch. "What is so complicated? I want to be there to help you." He took her hand in his.

"No. You don't need to be involved. It's just work stuff. I'll figure it out." Billie couldn't tell him that she was thirsty for blood. That she was obsessed with Phareed and punishing him.

She wasn't always obsessed with Phareed though. When Billie became an ADA she had finally gotten into position to avenge her father's death. For years she thought about becoming an attorney and prosecuting Kareem. She was consumed with it. The first thing she did after becoming an ADA was start trying to go after Kareem. But she quickly found out that Kareem had disappeared. For a while she'd been despondent over losing her opportunity to bring Kareem to justice after all these years. Sure, she found some pleasure in bringing other criminals to justice, but it felt as though her main goal, the only one she'd had for as long as she could remember, had been dashed.

It took an act of fate to focus her again. By chance one night she found herself in the company of one of the thugs who worked for Phareed, who'd taken over Kareem's territory. Revenge became all the sweeter when the game suddenly became about going after Kareem's heir, who was very much in the picture, and whose crew was just as dangerous and criminal.

"Billie." Walter pleaded with his eyes for her to let him help.

She looked into his eyes at the sincerity they conveyed and kissed him passionately. She could tell this caught him off guard, which made her even hornier for him. She slid her tongue between his teeth and moaned as he tugged on the back of her hair. "Fuck me! Fuck me hard," Billie shouted as she felt Walter's large erection pressing up against her body.

"Hold on, baby. I want to go slow," he said.

Given the adrenaline she had been feeling the entire day, she wasn't in the mood to take things slow, but decided not to bitch, as Walter had been upset with her earlier.

As Walter pulled her close again, Billie reached around and grabbed his tight ass. She had never felt an ass as hard as Walter's and she loved the feeling of it in her grasp. She slid her hands forward and unbuckled Walter's belt.

"Just relax," she said as she took off his pants. Walter's breathing became heavy as she licked his cock from top to bottom, teasing him. She loved playing this game.

All of a sudden Billie stood up.

"What are you—" Before Walter could even finish his sentence, Billie forcefully shoved his ass onto the couch. Without wasting one second, she started sucking his dick hard, grabbing his balls with one hand and playing with herself with the other.

"You like that, baby?" Billie said as she continued to shove his cock in her mouth.

Walter grabbed her chin, pulling it up so that her eyes could meet his. "You know what I like," he replied.

With that, Walter tore Billie's clothes off and bent her over on the couch. With one sharp thrust, he was inside of her body, feeling her tight pussy opening for him.

Billie yelled as he slammed his dick inside of her again, this time grabbing her hair and pulling it toward his body.

It was on. After more deep thrusts that Billie knew would leave her sore the next morning, Walter lifted Billie off the couch and playfully threw her over his shoulder.

"Hey!" Billie screamed as Walter ran into the bedroom. This was what Billie liked about Walter. He was such a serious and damned good detective, but could be so playful, just like how she remembered her father being as a little girl.

Anger took over her body as the memories of her father's murder were suddenly running through her mind. It was her turn to fuck Walter hard.

"I'm on top," Billie said, and Walter did not argue. She rode his cock harder than she had ever ridden it before. "Rub my clit while I fuck you!" she aggressively said to Walter.

"That's fucking hot, baby," Walter said as his mouth gaped open at her blatant aggression. "I'm going to cum soon."

"Don't you fucking think about it 'til I cum!" Billie shouted.

"Shit! A'ight, chill."

Billie fucked him faster and faster, rubbing her clit harder and harder.

"It's rising, it's rising!" Billie shuddered as she experienced a leg-shaking orgasm. Walter was so turned on by her finale that he gave her three more thrusts and then he came too.

"Damn, baby, I guess work has been stressful."

The two lovers lay in bed spent from their epic sex session.

Billie nuzzled into Walter and cupped his dick in her hands. "I love your cock."

"I do too. Saw some guy today got his dick chopped off. Never want that happening to me." He kissed Billie's forehead.

"That's gruesome. Why did they do that to him?" Billie acted like she was disgusted by the thought. She was thinking how perfect it was that she could now get information as to how much the police knew about her murder.

"Don't know. Normally I would think it was a jealous girlfriend, but this guy was just released from prison. No known girlfriend, wife, nothing."

"Strange."

"Yeah, thought maybe it was a prostitute, but we spoke to all the pimps we know, and none had any girls visit this dude."

"Why a prostitute?"

"We had a partial description of a woman leaving his home."

Billie's heart sank and her stomach filled with butterflies.

"What did she look like?" Billie tried to sound as casual as possible when asking the question, hoping Walter didn't sense her guilt.

"Don't really know. The eyewitness said it was hard to see. Only really gave us a description of her clothes. That's why we thought prostitute."

Billie calmed down a little but could still feel her heart beating fast. Billie didn't want Walter feeling her accelerated heartbeat so she rolled away from him to create a little space.

"Oh," was all she could answer.

"There have been two other murders recently that we think might be connected to this one, but this one is different. This one was just brutal. Much more violent than the others."

"Why?" Billie was going to try to get as much information as possible by saying as little as possible.

"Why was this more violent? We don't know."

"No; why do you think they are connected?"

"Oh, all three guys worked for this drug dealer, Phareed, and had been out of the pen for just a few days. We think Phareed is sending some sort of message, but the dick-chopping thing is throwing us off."

This was exactly what Billie wanted to hear. This had been her plan—start killing guys connected to Phareed to bring the heat on him. Not only did she want to kill Phareed, she wanted to bring down his organization. Bringing more attention to him would bring more attention to his organization, thus, hopefully, crushing it.

Before she'd had any plan—before, even, she'd decided to go after Phareed in Kareem's stead—Billie had once complained to Kevin that she thought no one was getting punished enough. He'd jokingly said to her, "What would be enough punishment? To kill them?"

This comment sparked up the light bulb in Billie's head. At first she didn't want to admit that the idea excited her, that she agreed it would be a fitting punishment. But the more she fantasized about it the more of a reality she thought it could become. But she still thought she could never go through with murdering someone.

Her first kill was, in fact, accidental. She had been walking home late one night after a fancy work function. She had been feeling good from the alcohol she had consumed and wanted to feel the air on her face, so she had decided to walk home.

*She stopped into a late-night deli to grab a bottle of water. As she walked in a guy was walking out.*

*"Mmm, you fine," he said as they passed each other.*

*Billie ignored him and kept walking.*

*When she walked back outside the guy was leaning against the wall, waiting for her.*

*"Hey, baby, you need an escort?" he asked as he sipped his beer from a paper bag.*

*Billie ignored him again and walked in the opposite direction from where he was standing.*

*"You too good for a nigga? You some sort of uppity bitch, huh?" he called to her.*

*She picked up her pace when she realized the guy was following her. Her heart beat faster, keeping time now with the click of her heels against the sidewalk; perspiration dotted her upper lip.*

*"Bitch, I'm talkin' to you. Don't fuckin' ignore me." He picked his pace up to match hers.*

*Billie was having trouble keeping the pace in her evening gown and high heels. She tried to remove her heels while still maintaining her rapid pace. If she could get her heels off she could run. She kicked one of them off, but her other heel was wedged in it too tightly for her to just slip out of it. She stumbled as she bent over to grab at it, wrenched it off her foot, and took a split second to regain her balance. She felt freedom, but then she felt the man grab her from behind.*

*"What's your problem bitch? I think I need to teach you a lesson." He covered her mouth so she couldn't scream. She struggled to get free as he pushed her toward an alley one building down.*

*The alley was a dead end in the middle of two commercial buildings. It was empty except for the garbage strewn everywhere. It smelled of urine and feces. It was obviously used by the homeless as a bathroom. Her bare feet scraped against pebbles, and a shard of broken glass sliced into her toe.*

*He forced her all the way to the end and forcefully pushed her against the wall. She hit the wall and fell to her knees. She was a little dazed from the impact. The guy was standing behind her as he started to undo his pants. She was on all fours attempting to get up when she saw an empty forty-ounce bottle in front of her. She lunged for it, and grabbed it around the neck. Just as she got to her feet the guy came toward her. She spun around and smashed the bottle into his face. The force of the blow sent him flailing backward. He tripped over some garbage and fell back. His body slammed into the ground and the back of his head violently cracked against the pavement.*

*Billie stood in shock, trembling, still holding the neck of the bottle. The rest of it had shattered on impact. She stared at the bloody face of her attacker and didn't know what to do. In a panic she ran. She wanted to get as far away from him before he had a chance to get up and come after her. She made it home still holding the bottleneck.*

*Billie tossed and turned all night thinking about what had happened. His voice was there with her, in the dark, every time she tried to close her eyes. She was afraid to report it because there was no way to prove that he attacked her. She could claim self-defense but it was his word against hers. She decided she would take her chances and keep quiet.*

*The next day at work Billie was reading the news online and came across a story about a guy who had just gotten out of prison and was found dead in an alley. He had apparently been beaten and his skull was cracked. They weren't sure if he died from the blow to his head or if he choked on his own blood.*

*Reading that the guy had died stunned Billie. Her heart actually skipped a beat when she read that he was dead. Her first reaction was terror. She thought for sure she was going to get arrested. But after she thought about it for a few more minutes her reaction turned to delight.* The scumbag got what he deserved. *Knowing that she had killed this guy empowered her. She had never felt this much a sense of accomplishment and satisfaction when she punished criminals legally. To Billie, this seemed a far more appropriate punishment.*

*Billie immediately did some research on the guy and it turned out that he had been associated with Phareed's crew. This, then, set Billie on her new path: to target guys associated with Phareed.*

*After a few weeks had gone by Billie felt secure that she had gotten away with murder. She couldn't believe how easy it was and she began seriously thinking*

*about taking the law into her own hands. She realized
it was the only way to truly avenge her father's death.*

The sound of Walter's voice brought Billie back to
the present. "We would love to arrest this Phareed guy,
but he is bulletproof. He runs everything and has set
it up so he is so protected and removed from it all. We
can't get anything on this guy."

Billie's jaw tightened. Thinking about Phareed and
hearing how protected he was enraged her. He was
protected from the law but not from street justice. The
solution to the problem of Phareed was so obvious to
Billie. *Just kill him and then you are done with him.*
Billie thought it was even easier for the police because
they had a license to kill. They could easily go after
him, shoot him, and then say they thought he had a
gun. *Most likely he probably would be carrying a gun,*
thought Billie.

"Just fucking arrest him!" she burst out. What she
was really thinking was, *just fucking kill him.*

Walter looked at Billie and chuckled at her inten-
sity. "I wish we could, baby, but we have nothing." He
kissed her cheek then walked to the bathroom.


As Walter snored lightly, Billie stared into the shad-
ows playing against the bedroom walls. She spent the
night, until well near dawn, thinking about Phareed
and how she was going to make him pay.

# Chapter 5

The air in the back room of the strip club, Honey Trap, was thick with weed smoke. It was late on a Friday night and the room was packed. Corner boys, pimps, businessmen, and, of course, strippers all partied and danced to the thumping hip-hop bass being blasted by the DJ.

Phareed swirled the dice in his right hand. "Money on the floor!" he yelled.

There was an instant swirl of action around him. Men were throwing money on the floor, yelling out bets. Others were making side bets with each other. When all the bets had been made, Phareed threw the dice to start another game of Ci-Lo. The game was fast and furious as money was being thrown down and picked up. The dice, thrown against the wall, seemed like an endless loop that constantly elicited some huge reaction from the crowd.

"Nigga, nobody can beat me at Ci-Lo." Phareed took a hit from the blunt he was holding, and his chest, already swollen with muscles and pride, puffed out even more. He threw the dice again—another winning roll. He scooped up the money lying in front of him.

"I'm out." He stuffed the cash in his pocket. His declaration elicited a moan from the crowd. Some guys were winning and wanted him to keep throwing, and others were just trying to kiss his ass and wanted to make him feel good. This was the life of Phareed—partying, making money, and traveling with an entourage who would do anything for him. He owned the Philadelphia streets, and if anyone challenged that, they were never heard from again.

Phareed had inherited his empire from the notorious Philly gangster Kareem Fahmy, who had built his empire from nothing. Phareed had started as a lowly corner boy for Kareem but quickly worked his way up to his most trusted lieutenant. Kareem treated Phareed like his son, and when he was ready he handed Phareed the keys to his empire. Kareem took off for the good life on a Caribbean island. He was still counseling Phareed, and Phareed had to pass all decisions by Kareem, but Kareem's plan was to lay low and have Phareed be the figurehead of the network. Kareem knew that everyone was always gunning for the top guy, so if he made it look like Phareed was the top dog he would be safe.

With Phareed as the head, the network expanded its distribution and diversified their operation. They now controlled the drug trade in Philly, they had the pimp game on lock, he supplied most illegal guns, and now, with the opening of the Honey Trap, they were opening legit businesses for money laundering. Phareed had big plans for his empire.

Phareed puffed on his blunt as he walked through the crowd, searching for a nice little ho to grind up on. All the girls were doing everything they could to catch his eye. Phareed looked, but not of them was doing it for him. He had already fucked most of these broads, and the ones he hadn't were busted. They were the ones he had on payroll for the freaks who came to his club and liked their hoes a little deformed—super fat, anorexic, or possibly pregnant. Phareed liked his women tight and thick.

Not really seeing anything that made his dick twitch, Phareed went out to the main room of the club in search of a thick-ass ho who he'd had fun with in the past. That room was just as packed as the back room. Phareed liked what he saw. All these heads up in the club meant one thing: more money.

"Isis." Phareed stood at the edge of the stage.

The dancer was bent over in a dude's face, taking his money and making his mouth water. She was locked in on this sucker and didn't hear Phareed over the loud music.

"Isis!" Phareed yelled louder.

This time she heard him.

"Hey, daddy." She smiled as she slinked her way to him. She bent down from the stage and gave Phareed a kiss on his cheek, then licked his earlobe.

"You done dancing for tonight." He pulled out $1,000 from his pocket and handed it to Isis. "You with me for the rest of the night."

He helped her off the stage and took her to the party going on in the back room. Isis grabbed herself a glass of Moët and sat on one of the couches. On the glass banquet table in front of her was a pile of cocaine. She placed her champagne down, rolled up one of the bills that Phareed had given her, and snorted a big fat line of coke. She rose from her leaned position, and her eyes were big as saucers.

Phareed laughed when he saw the look in her eyes. *This bitch just got high as shit,* he thought. *She ready to party.*

"Come here," he said, standing on the opposite side of the banquet table.

She leaned forward, did another quick hit of coke, and purred, "Let's party, motherfucker," as she came up from the coke, wiping her nose.

Phareed had this bitch grinding up on him in the middle of the dance floor. The coke and weed had them both feeling nice, and the bass bumping from the speakers had them in a smooth grinding rhythm. His hands roamed her curvaceous body. She had him so ready to fuck that his dick was bulging through his jeans. Isis was ready to get down too when she felt the monster hiding in his pants rubbing against her pussy. She remembered how much fun she had with Phareed the last time. *I'm gonna fuck this nigga good and become his main bitch,* she thought.

"Let's go somewhere more private," she said.

"You read my mind." Phareed grabbed her and pulled her to his office. His boy Jumbo was standing at the door.

"No one comes in here," Phareed said to Jumbo.

"A'ight." The 300-pound monster took his position as gatekeeper.

Phareed and Isis walked into the office ready to get their freak, but were surprised when they saw Stone sitting behind Phareed's desk.

Stone was Phareed's right-hand man. Phareed had the street smarts and the tactical shit on lock, but Stone was straight-up business. He was the numbers nigga. The man was a genius at laundering money.

"Yo." Phareed stopped in his tracks.

"Yo. Just got off the phone wit' my man."

"A'ight. Now bounce. I need this joint for a minute." Phareed motioned to the door with his head.

"Nah. I think we need to speak for a minute first."

"That shit can wait." Phareed brushed him off.

"Nah, real talk. You should hear this."

Phareed sighed. "Shit. A'ight." He turned to Isis. "Wait outside."

She turned and walked out without saying a word. Isis was disappointed, but she wasn't going to let it show. She was angling to be his bitch and didn't want to seem whiny. If she had to, she would wait all night.

"Hit me. What's up?" Phareed said after Isis closed the door.

"My man just told me that Ramon was murked last night."

"Who?" Phareed asked.

"That Spanish nigga from around the way. He did a bid for you up in Frackville."

"Yeah, so what? That nigga is nothin' to me. Some low-level earner."

"I know, but this nigga just got out the pen and someone did him. That shit is happening with frequency. One of our workers gets out of lockup and next thing you know . . . *Pow,* that nigga dead."

Phareed thought about this for a second. "You think someone tryin'a send a message?"

"For sure. I think someone is coming after your ass. This shit is too coincidental."

"Word." Phareed shook his head as he thought about who might be making a move on him.

"And get this shit: they chopped his dick off. That's some message-sending shit if I ever heard it."

"Damn. You ain't lie." Phareed subconsciously grabbed at his own dick. The second he touched himself, he remembered why he was in the office in the first place. "I don't need to be thinkin' about this right now. I got some pussy to pound. Fuck. Put word out on the street and find out what sick fuck is doing all this killin'."

"One more thing," Stone said. "My man said that the cops are thinking it might be you ordering the hits. They might start puttin' more heat on us."

"Fuck them. Dumb muthafuckin' five-oh. Just find out who's doin' this shit and bring them to me."

"A'ight." Stone walked out.

As Stone opened the door, Phareed yelled, "Isis, get your ass in here and suck my dick."

She appeared instantly, prepared to please her man.

# Chapter 6

Billie arrived at her office the next morning a little sore between her legs. It was a nice little reminder of her night with Walter.

She sat at her desk and began the process of sifting through files. After several hours of research her eyes were watered and blurry from looking at her computer. She hadn't found anything that could even remotely start a case. She was frustrated to say the least. Using the law to punish criminals was tedious and useless. Billie was having trouble even faking that she enjoyed the work, that she took any satisfaction in it. There was only one way that Billie was sure that criminals were being punished correctly.

Billie pushed away from her desk and leaned back in her chair. She changed her focus to more important things, like Phareed. Getting close to him seemed damn near impossible. She could help Walter investigate him and hopefully find some way to go after him, but that could take a long time. It was how the old Billie would handle the situation. The new Billie wanted to take immediate action. No wasting time with arguments in a courtroom convincing a jury to find him guilty, then giving him some bullshit little sentence. Billie's wanted to bring the hammer of justice down on him in her own way.

She sat up in her seat with an interesting thought. What if she could find a way to get close to this guy and take him down from the inside? Instead of going after him in a roundabout way she could go after him directly. She did it with the other three men she killed, so why not Phareed? The old Billie was intent on getting him in a courtroom and putting him behind bars. She wanted him to look her in the eyes as she slew him in court and brought him to justice. Now she wanted him to look her in the eye while she was literally slaying him.

Billie smiled as she thought about a new plan of attack. "Time to go hunting," she whispered.

Billie printed out all the files regarding Phareed and his associates. She stuffed them all into a folder and placed it in her briefcase. Even though it was hardly the afternoon, she was done working for the day.

"Hey, Billie, where you going?" Kevin asked as she passed him in the hall.

"Lunch." She kept walking.

"Great. I'll tag along. I'm starved." He reversed his direction and began walking beside her.

"This is a personal lunch. You're not invited," she coldly stated.

"Well, fuck you too." He frowned.

She stopped instantly and shot daggers at him with her eyes. She was about to go off on him but stopped herself and thought better of it. Instead she remained silent and continued walking out of the building. She had more important things to deal with than dealing with a white boy whose feelings were hurt.

She didn't really have much of a plan when she pulled out into the heavy downtown traffic. All she knew was that she was seeking justice and it would be served. Billie began cruising around some of the worst neighborhoods in Philadelphia, hoping that she would see Phareed. After an hour of endless driving she realized this was a complete waste of her time. She wasn't going to miraculously run into him by coincidence. She needed to make it happen for certain. She needed to know where he laid his head, where he liked to party, where he conducted his business.

Billie turned back to one of the streets where she had seen some corner boys working the block. She was going to get some answers.

As Billie turned on to the block, she saw the same boys still hustling. She slowly pulled up to the corner and stopped in front of the group of boys. Each boy in the group was wearing the same oversized white T-shirt and jeans halfway down their asses. It was their uniform. The only thing that set them apart from one another was their shoes. Some wore Timberlands, others wore Nikes.

She lowered her window and motioned for one of the boys. The youngest of the bunch started toward her car, but before he could make any progress the oldest pulled him back by his shirt.

"I got this," the oldest said. He approached Billie's car and leaned into the passenger side window.

"What you need, beautiful? I'm always ready to help a lovely lady."

Billie smiled at the young boy's attempt to charm her. Looking at his smooth face, Billie figured he was no more than sixteen. *Still a baby,* she thought.

"How cute that you are so charming. You can help me by telling me where I can find Phareed."

"What? I ain't good enough for you?" the boy asked.

"You are fine, young one. I just need Phareed."

"A'ight. I hear you. Give me fifty and I'll tell you where you can find that nigga."

"You want fifty dollars?" Billie sounded incredulous.

The boy just smiled and shrugged his shoulders.

"Fine." She reached in her purse and produced fifty dollars.

The boy snatched it from her and counted it before putting it in his pocket.

"Fuck you, bitch. Get the fuck out my block." He pushed away from the car and walked back to his boys. They greeted each other with ritualistic hand slaps and laughed as the young boy told them what he did to Billie.

She sat steaming in the car as she watched them laughing at her expense. It took all of her control not to jump out and go after the boy. Figuring at least one of the boys had a gun, she thought better and just mean mugged them from her car.

Seeing Billie still on the block, the boy yelled out, "What I say? Leave, bitch." He pulled up his shirt to expose the gun in his waistband.

Seeing that she was correct about the gun, Billie put the car in drive and got the fuck out of there.

"Fuck!" She slammed her hands on the steering wheel. She needed a different approach if she was going to get any information about Phareed from any of his workers.

She drove until she found another group of corner boys, and just like the previous time she pulled right up to them. One of them came over immediately and leaned in her window. "What you need?"

"I need some information."

"I don't sell no information, pig." He walked back to his position on the corner.

*Shit. He thought I was a cop.* Another wasted effort. How was she going to get these young bucks to tell her what she needed? She drove off in search of another corner boy. As she drove the dirty streets, she brainstormed how she was going to get any of these kids to talk. All afternoon, she rolled through the poverty-stricken neighborhoods and watched the action on the sidewalks—groups of men gathering in front of buildings telling grand stories that were only partly true, women walking to the bodegas carrying a child in one arm and dragging their older sibling with the other. This was the life that Billie had grown up with. She was familiar with these scenes. She loved her city, but she hated most of its residents. She turned up the music in her car to drown out the neighborhood noises until she could find what she was looking for.

She pulled down a rather deserted street except for some women loitering near the middle of the block. As she drove past, she saw that they were prostitutes waiting for a john. An idea popped into her head.

The next dope boys she found, she again pulled right up to them. Like clockwork, the minute the car stopped a boy approached. Billie thought that they seemed like trained dogs responding to a whistle.

"What you need?" This boy seemed a little older than the others she had run into. Billie guessed him to be around nineteen years old.

"I need your help. I need you to act like my pimp."

"What the fuck? You serious?" The boy chuckled.

"Some guy I fucked a few days ago is harassing me. I want nothing to do with this buster, so I told him my pimp won't let me see anyone. I need you to stand in as my pimp."

"You ain't dressed like no ho." He said with some caution in his voice.

"I'm high end. I'm not some streetwalking bitch."

The boy smiled. "Yeah, I like that. Whatever you need, ma."

"Good. Get in."

"Hold on, ma. What's in it for me?" He ogled Billie.

"I'll give you fifty dollars."

"Make it a hundred."

She eyed him for a moment, wary after having just been ripped off. Then, realizing she had little choice, she snapped open her purse and dug out the bills. "Fine. Whatever." She handed him the money.

"That's a start. Now how about a little somethin' else?" He gave her his best seductive look.

Billie couldn't believe all these boys on the streets trying to act like men. She could just tell that this kid had no idea how to seduce a woman and everything he was trying he learned from television. She almost felt bad for him. Then she remembered he was a drug dealer ruining her city.

She needed him, though, so she played along. With a seductive look of her own she said, "We'll see what we can work out, young'un."

That was enough of a yes for the boy. He jumped into the passenger seat, leaving the rest of his posse on the corner.

Billie quickly pulled away from the curb, making sure she kept the boy in the confined space. The anticipation she started to feel about getting her information had adrenaline coursing through her veins.

"You in a hurry," the boy commented.

Billie didn't realize, but the adrenaline was causing her to really step on the gas and speed down the street. As soon as the boy pointed it out, she eased off on the gas pedal.

"Oh, yeah. Sorry. I guess I'm just excited about getting this guy off my back," she said.

"Who is this nigga?"

"Just some guy I met at a bar. I wouldn't be having this problem if I was in Phareed's stable of women."

"Why you ain't with Phareed? That's where you make the money."

"That's what everybody keeps tellin' me, but no one will introduce me. I'm new to the city. Just moved here from Pittsburgh."

"Shit. That's what you want I'll take you to Phareed. Me and that nigga is tight."

"Really?" Billie couldn't believe her luck.

"Yeah. I'll take you to him now."

"Just tell me where to go."

The young man directed Billie on to South Columbus Boulevard. They headed south, passing the *USS United States* and then taking a left onto South Columbus Avenue. They drove parallel to the river for a little while.

"Pull in here." He pointed to a parking lot on the left.

Billie followed his directions. They passed an empty trailer as they drove through the open chain-link gates. Billie looked at the young man with uncertainty on her face.

The young man smiled at her. "Keep going." He pointed straight ahead.

Determined to finally meet Phareed, Billie obeyed and drove slowly across the expansive parking lot, heading toward the Delaware River. Close to the end of the parking lot there was a dirt road to the left that Billie was instructed to turn down.

The sun had finally set, and Billie turned on her headlights. As soon as her lights illuminated the darkness and she pulled onto the dirt road, she saw a rusty old water tower rising in front of her. Getting a bad feeling, she stopped the car.

"Where are you taking me?" She looked at the young man.

Before she knew what was happening, the young man punched her in the face, snapping her head in the opposite direction. Blood immediately started flowing from her split lip.

"Bitch. I ain't gonna act like your pimp. I am your pimp. You my bitch now." He threw a series of heavy blows to the back of Billie's head, causing her to see stars. She fought to stop herself from passing out as she covered up to protect herself from his vicious punches. The moment there was a pause in the onslaught from the young man, Billie opened the car door and ran.

"Bitch!" The young man jumped out and chased after Billie.

Billie ran for her life toward the water tower. She looked back and saw the man was in pursuit and gaining quickly. Billie tripped as she turned back around, and fell into the bushes in front of the water tower. In a matter of seconds the man was on top of her, sitting on her back, pinning her face into the dirt.

"You feisty, huh, bitch? You like to play?" He punched the back of her head.

Billie could feel the tears streaming down her face and mixing with the blood from her lip. She struggled to get free from the grasp of the young man, but he was too strong. She could feel the full weight of him on her back as he used his knees to pin her arms down. Dirt was flying into her mouth, causing her to choke as she screamed, "Fuck you! Get off me! Help!" She was in panic mode.

"I'm gonna teach my bitch to obey. You behave and I'll take care of you." He grabbed a hold of the waistband of her slacks and yanked them down, exposing her bare ass. She struggled even more now, violently trying to get out from under him. The pain in her arms from the pressure of his knees was becoming unbearable. She struggled desperately to free her arms. During her struggle, she felt her left hand hit something hard. She looked and saw a rock about an inch from her fingertips.

"Yeah. I'm gonna tear this ass up." He started unbuckling his pants.

Billie strained to stretch her fingers and grab the rock. Her fingertips were barely making contact with it. The young man moved into position to ram his penis into her. The moment he released her arms from under his knees, Billie grabbed the rock and was able to swing around and smash the rock in his face. The force of the blow knocked him off of Billie, and she was able to scramble to her feet. The young man was momentarily stunned, allowing Billie enough time to wind up and bash the rock into his head.

"You motherfucker!" she screamed as she repeatedly slammed the rock into his head. The young man's face split open like a coconut with blood pouring out of the gashes she was creating. She kept on smashing until she was too tired to swing anymore. Then she collapsed to her knees and sobbed.

After a while, she was able to compose herself and stop crying. She pulled her pants back up but had to leave them unfastened. The button and zipper had been ripped off so she was unable to fasten them. The young man's body lay motionless beside her.

Billie stood over the bloody body and stared down at her would-be rapist. She thought back to her very first kill, and how the episode changed her. Now this kill transformed her even more. She could feel it. She felt stronger both physically and mentally.

Before getting back into her car, Billie walked to the edge of the Delaware River and threw the rock as far as she could. She then kneeled at the shoreline and washed the blood from her hands and face.

What she couldn't wash away was the memory of what just happened. She replayed the attack over and over during the drive back to her home.

Billie pulled up to a red light. Across the street she saw a bright neon sign that said NINA'S BAR. With memories of her father's murder and her recent attack dancing in her head, she decided to drown them out with a couple of drinks at the bar. She crossed the intersection and pulled into a parking space in front of Nina's bar.

Billie walked into the dark bar, which stank of stale beer that smelled about a hundred years old. A lone pool table sat in the far corner, and music played on a busted radio behind the bar. This was hardly Billie's style, but all she wanted was what the rest of the handful of patrons seemed to want: a hard drink, and fast.

"What can I get you?" the bartender asked as Billie took a stool directly in front of him.

"Grey Goose on the rocks," she said.

The bartender paused before starting to make the drink. The order surprised him. Normally his customers asked for the cheapest beer or liquor.

While he was pouring the vodka, Billie looked at her reflection in the mirror behind the bar. What she saw staring back at her shocked her. Her lip was already swollen, and there was dried blood all around the wound. She had scrapes on her forehead and her hair was a bird's nest. Obviously the water at the river only spread the blood and didn't do a decent job of cleaning it off.

"Where's the bathroom?" she asked the bartender.

He pointed toward the back of the bar, unfazed by how she looked. This was the type of bar where he saw all sorts of messed-up shit walking through the doors.

Billie locked the bathroom door behind her and stood in front of the sink. She pumped the decrepit soap dispenser until she got a few bubbles of pink goo, and began cleaning her face. Her head was throbbing from the impact of her attacker's punches. The warm water was so soothing that she wanted to jump in the sink and soak for hours, and she hardly cared how rusty it looked. The first thing she was going to do when she got home was run a nice hot bath.

She started to reconsider her decision to stop for a drink. The bath sounded much better all of a sudden. She dried her face with a few paper towels from the roll, fixed her hair, and went back to the bar. She would have this one drink then hit the road.

"You want some ice cubes to put on that lip?" The bartender held out a plastic bag filled with ice.

"Sure." She pressed the bag against her mouth. The coldness on her lip felt just as soothing as the warm water had.

Billie finally took a good look at the bar she was in. It was dark and it was depressing. She fit right in with the rest of the customers drowning their emotions. This wasn't the type of bar where people came to party. They came to forget their problems, to escape their troubles. Billie was definitely done after one drink. She would rather be at home in a hot bubble bath drinking a nice glass of red wine.

There was nothing Billie wanted to look at in this bar, so she decided it best to just stare into her glass. The ice cubes were more interesting to her than the sad patrons in their alcoholic haze.

"What's up, Stone?" The bartender slid a bottle of Heineken toward the man who sat next to Billie.

Billie slightly turned her head and looked out the corner of her eyes to see the man. Her heart skipped a beat when she saw his face. She couldn't believe her luck. It was Phareed's right-hand man, sitting next to her at the worst dive bar in all of Philadelphia. She knew him from mug shots for various petty crimes, all of which he was able to get out of.

Billie felt her pulse speed up and her palms get sweaty. She took a sip of her vodka to calm her nerves. She placed the bag of ice next to her on the bar, took one more sip, and then turned toward Stone.

"Hi." She smiled as warmly as she could for a woman with a busted lip.

"Hi." He sipped his beer. "You should keep the ice on that lip."

"I'm good. It looks worse than it is. I'm Sheila." She put her hand out.

"Stone." He took her hand. "What happened?"

"Oh, I got jumped by some kids. No big deal. They got like fifty bucks."

"What the fuck is wrong with kids these days? Hearing that shit makes me angry."

"It's fine, really." She smiled. "What happened to you?"

"What you mean?"

"Well, I'm here to forget I got jumped, but why would a fine man like you be in a depressing bar like this?"

"I like to come in here when I'm stressed and I need to get away. No one bothers me in here." He sipped his beer. "And I own the place." He smiled.

"Oh, a businessman," she said in a flirty way.

"Something like that."

"What's that mean?"

"Well, I work for someone else. This place is my own thing. Make a few extra dollars on the side."

"I like that. A man who isn't afraid to get his." She put her hand on his shoulder.

Stone took a real look at Billie. Despite the busted lip, this woman was fine. She had a class about her that he found intriguing. "What's your story, ma?"

"You know . . . just moved here from Pittsburgh, looking for work."

"I know some niggas from out that way. They in Braddock."

"Yeah, I know Braddock. I'm from the Hill."

He shook his head. "What work you do?"

"Whatever I can right now."

"What's your dream job? I know a lot of people. I might be able to help." If it helped him get in her pants, he would get her any job she wanted.

"I'm good at public relations. I'm also thinking I might want to go to law school."

*Two things I'm always in need of. This is a classy bitch,* he thought.

"Big ambitions. I like that," he said.

Billie was feeling at ease now. She was ready to play this nigga like a fiddle. Men were so easy. All you had to do was give them the hope of sex and they were putty in your hand.

"So? If you help me, what can I do to repay you?" She seductively rubbed his inner thigh.

His dick sprang to attention. "You wanna get outta here, ma? Head back to my place?"

She removed her hand from his thigh. "I'm a good girl. I don't sleep with a guy on the first date."

"You call this a date?" he asked.

"What else is it?"

"I'll show you a first date. Come out with me right now."

"Not tonight. I just got jumped. I'm a little raw. I should head home." She put her hand back on his thigh. "Give me your number. I'll call you."

He grabbed a napkin, wrote his number down, and handed it to her. "You better be calling me."

"Don't you worry about that, Stone. You'll be seeing me again, for sure." She put the napkin in her purse, kissed him on his cheek, and walked out of the bar.

"Damn." Stone watched her walk away.

All the aches and pains Billie had been feeling when she entered the bar disappeared. The bath she was about to take was now a celebratory bath and not one to soak her wounds. Billie was feeling like fate was shining down on her from the heavens. She looked up to the heavens and knew that her daddy was looking back at her. He was definitely watching over her and had a hand in her chance encounter with Stone.

# Chapter 7

"What happened to you?" Walter asked with concern. He had just entered the restaurant where he was meeting Billie. It had been a few days since her attack, and there were still signs from the beating she took. She had been calling out sick to work and wouldn't go back until she had healed, but she figured she couldn't keep avoiding Walter.

Billie remained sitting at the booth she was in. "It's nothing."

"Bullshit it's nothing." He sat across from Billie. "You're bruised and your lip was busted. Tell me what happened."

"I got jumped by some kids. I'm fine." She placed her hand over his as a sign of reassurance.

"What did they look like?"

"I don't really know. I wasn't too concerned with their appearance."

"Do you remember anything? Their clothes?"

"I don't know . . . the same thing they all wear. Over-sized white T-shirts and baggy jeans." Billie was going to be as vague as possible. She didn't want Walter to start investigating.

"Where did it happen?"

"Um, over on Cushing Hill and South Street."

"Little motherfuckers," he mumbled.

"It's okay. Let's just enjoy our meal." She placed her menu in front of him, hoping to distract him from the conversation.

"Fine." He started to look through the menu, but quickly put it down. He wasn't finished asking questions. "Did you file a report?"

"Baby, can we drop it? I don't want to think about it."

"Billie, you gotta be kidding me. You didn't file a report?"

"No. I don't want to talk about this anymore. It's over. I'm fine. Drop it." There was anger in her voice.

Walter got the hint. He was disappointed that she didn't report the attack, but he was going to try not to push her any further. He told himself to drop it for now while they were eating, but someone was going to pay for hurting his Billie.

But when the waiter came over, and Billie ordered the grilled chicken breast, Walter couldn't help himself from snorting.

"Excuse me," said Billie. "Do you have something to say about my order?"

"No. I mean, if you want to go ahead and order the chicken, then you're going to order the chicken. Nothing's gonna stop you, even though everyone knows you come here for the burgers."

"Well, I don't want a burger. I have been ordering my food for some time now, Walter, and I think I know how to handle myself."

"By all means, don't let me interrupt."

"Fine," said Billie through gritted teeth. "I won't."

Walter grinned at the waiter. "*I*, of course, will have a burger. *I* know the proper protocol for things, and *I* know that when you come here, you order a burger."

Billie gave him a cool stare. "Real men eat chicken."

"Excuse me?"

The waiter just stood there, utterly confused. When the two patrons in front of him stopped bickering, and just stared daggers at each other, he rushed off to put their orders in, afraid to stick around any longer.

Most of the meal was silent after that, but for the clinking of silverware. When they were almost finished eating, Billie decided to try conversation again.

"How's your new partner?" she asked.

"Huh?" Walter wasn't listening. His mind had wandered from the attack Billie had just dealt him to the attack Billie had endured. He was fuming inside and couldn't shake it. "Oh, yeah, um, he's good."

"So? When do I meet him?"

"Look, Billie, I gotta go. Really busy at work right now." Walter was so heated about her attack he couldn't sit there any longer. He was going crazy on the inside thinking about Billie getting jumped. He put cash on the table for their meal, gave her a kiss, and bolted out the door.

Walter got into his car and headed directly to the corner of Cushing Hill and South Street. The corner was a notorious spot for young hoodlums and gangbangers. The Cushing Hill Gang had been running that corner since the seventies. In recent years they had begun working with Phareed, and their drug operation had multiplied.

Walter drove down Cushing Hill ready to take out his aggressions on the young corner boys. When he was in sight of South Street he stepped on the gas and sped right up onto the curb. Everyone on the corner started scattering in all directions.

Walter jumped out of the car and began chasing the nearest kid around the corner onto South Street. The chubby little boy was already struggling to run, holding his baggy jeans up with one hand and shooting panicked looks over his shoulder, and he hadn't even made it half a block when Walter easily caught up with him. Walter grabbed his shoulders and tossed him up against the wall. Before the boy knew what was happening, he was handcuffed with his face smashed against a brick wall.

"You like to beat up women?" Walter smashed the boy's face even harder into the wall.

"The fuck you talkin' about? Get the fuck off me!" He spoke out of the side of his mouth that was not getting flattened by the wall.

"You know exactly what I'm talking about, you little fucker." Walter began patting him down.

"Nigga, leave me alone. I didn't do shit."

"Oh, no? Well, I know that someone on this corner jumped a woman, so now you gonna pay unless you tell me who did it."

"I don't know what the fuck you talking about, pig."

Walter again aggressively pushed the boy's face into the wall. "No? Well, we're going down to the station."

Walter held up a dime bag that he had found in the boy's pocket. "Maybe then you'll know what I'm talkin' about."

"Whatever. You can't scare me. I'm underage, nigga. I won't do shit for time for that scrap of weed."

Walter grabbed the boy and dragged him back to his car. He shoved the chubby little shit into the back seat then drove to the station house.

"Nigga, this shit is pointless. Phareed gonna make sure I'm out before you can dot your I's and cross them T's."

"You need to watch your mouth!" Hearing this boy use Phareed's name angered Walter even more.

Walter pulled the boy into the station house and shoved him onto the nearest bench. "Put this fat little fuck into holding," Walter instructed one of the rookie officers at the desk. He then proceeded back to the detectives' area to find D'Angelo sitting at his desk on the phone.

"Let's go," Walter said to D'Angelo.

D'Angelo motioned to the phone to let Walter know he couldn't get up and go at that exact moment.

"Tell them you'll call them back. Let's go," Walter repeated.

D'Angelo shook his head in frustration. "Can I call you back later? I have a situation over here." D'Angelo listened to the caller's answer. "Okay. I'll call you back. Bye." He hung up the phone. "Damn, what?"

"We're going to talk to Phareed."

"Did we get a warrant?"

"No. We're going to happen to bump into him. I'm sick of this motherfucker thinking he runs this city."

"I don't know . . ." D'Angelo said uncertainly.

Walter planted his hands on his hips. "What the fuck don't you know? We're going to keep coming down on him until he makes a mistake. Now, come on." Walter headed out of the stationhouse. D'Angelo shook his head and followed his partner.

Walter and D'Angelo sat in their Crown Victoria in front of the Honey Trap. This was the boring part of the job—waiting. Walter wanted to kick down the door to the club and start busting heads, but he knew better. Yeah, he could walk into the club, act like a patron, and start asking questions, but no one would talk, or somehow some sleazy lawyer would say he needed a warrant to enter the premises. *Fuck that,* Walter thought. He would just wait Phareed out.

"What exactly do we expect to get out of this?" D'Angelo asked.

"To piss Phareed off and let him know I'm coming."

"You think that's the best way to take him down? Let him know who you are and what you plan to do?"

"The old way ain't working. It's time to change the game. This shit has become personal." Walter didn't take his eyes off the entrance to the Honey Trap.

"It never turns out good when you let your personal emotions take over," D'Angelo warned

"There he is." Walter hopped out of the car and made a beeline for Phareed. D'Angelo reluctantly followed his partner.

"Yo, my man." Walter came up behind Phareed.

Phareed and Jumbo quickly turned when they heard the footsteps behind them. Jumbo reached into his coat pocket for his pistol.

"Whoa." Walter held up his hands as he continued approaching.

Phareed and Jumbo stood their ground waiting for the stranger to approach. "The fuck you want?" Phareed said.

"I just want to ask a few questions." Walter was trying to be as calm as possible.

"Fuck you. I don't speak to no cop." Phareed could smell a cop a mile away. This nigga had cop all over him.

"What you know about the murders of your people recently?" Walter stood face to face with Phareed. D'Angelo stood off to the side.

"Don't know what you talkin' about," Phareed said calmly.

"No? The three men all murdered days after their release? All associates of yours?"

"Nigga, I don't know nothin'. I'm a legit businessman. If anyone has been murdered, that's too bad for them, but I ain't had nothin' to do with it."

"Really? So it's just a coincidence that they all have connections to you?" Walter was letting his anger seep through.

"That's what I'm sayin'." Phareed grinned.

The two men stared each other down, each one waiting for the other to make a move. The tension was extreme.

"What's up with your bitch over there? He don't like to talk?" Phareed motioned to D'Angelo with a nod.

"I'm asking the questions. I just want you to know I'm coming for you, motherfucker, so get used to this face. You're going to be seeing a lot of me."

"Bring it on. Like I said, I'm a legit businessman. I don't get down with the murder game. In fact, we in front of my business now. Why don't you and your bitch take these and go in and have yourself some fun. Seems like y'all need to relax." He pulled out some VIP passes and some Honey Trap dollars and held them out for Walter to take.

"I'm coming for you." Walter turned back to his car.

"Bye, ladies," Phareed called out to Walter and D'Angelo. He and Jumbo laughed as they watched the two detectives walk back to their car.

Walter slammed his car door. "I'm gonna get that motherfucker."

# Chapter 8

"Yo, meet me at the spot," Phareed said into the phone and hung up.

Stone tossed his cell phone next to him on the couch. He had hoped for a night in, watching the 76ers make their run to the playoffs. Stone decided he would watch the remaining five minutes of the quarter before heading out to meet with Phareed. He put his feet up on the coffee table, leaned back on the couch, and sipped his Heineken. He was in no rush to go and problem solve right now.

The first quarter ended with the Sixers leading by seven. Stone grudgingly turned his eighty-inch HDTV off. He looked out his penthouse window down on to Philadelphia. From that vantage point he felt like he owned the city. Maybe he could never actually own it, but some days he felt like he ran it. Even though Phareed was the head of the organization, Stone felt that without him the organization wouldn't be as strong. He was happy to stay behind the scenes as number two. The way Stone saw it, he was the brain, and Phareed was the face and muscle.

Stone picked up his keys and headed out of his penthouse to his Escalade in the parking lot.

He had his stereo bumping some Lil Wayne as he crossed the bridge into Camden, a shitty town just over the border in New Jersey. Phareed and Stone would meet at an abandoned warehouse along the river.

Stone drove his Escalade into the empty space. Phareed was already waiting, leaning up against his Hummer and texting.

After exiting his truck, Stone slid the massive steel door of the warehouse closed.

"What's good?" Stone said as the two men greeted each other by grabbing hands and bro-hugging each other.

"All good." Phareed leaned back on his Hummer. "Yo, what you find out about them murders?"

"We comin' up empty. Ain't no one know shit."

"You need to step your shit up then," Phareed shot back.

Stone wanted to say "fuck off," but he bit his tongue. He instead said, "I got a lotta niggas out there with their ear to the ground. No one's talkin'."

He hated when Phareed would question his work ethic. Stone was always making sure his business was being handled and he thought Phareed should know and respect that shit.

"Well, get more niggas out there and make niggas talk."

Again, Stone bit his tongue. He didn't see Phareed doing anything about the problem so for him to get a bug up his ass pissed Stone off. "Phareed, we start taking niggas off the corners it's gonna hurt business."

"The ones who stay on the corners have to sell more. So what? I want whoever this bitch is killing niggas." Phareed didn't want to hear excuses, he just wanted results and right now none were being produced.

"A'ight. I don't know if that's the best play though. We'll find out who it is. Someone is bound to talk," Stone said.

"I don't care what you think. Make 'em talk sooner rather than later."

This did not sit well with Stone. It was a slap in the face to him. He was loyal to Phareed and had always given him solid advice. He hoped that Phareed wasn't becoming too much of a playboy nigga. If that turned out to be the case he might have to reconsider his loyalties.

"A'ight. That it?" Stone kept it simple. He didn't want to keep talkin' about this shit. He was doin' what he was supposed to be doin'.

Phareed changed the subject. "You talk to your man lately?"

"Nah. No reason. Said he'd call when he got anything new."

"You need to call his ass. I had a visit from some gung-ho detective. Got all up in my grill askin' me 'bout them murders."

"That's why you stressin' this shit." Stone shook his head, showing he understood. Now Phareed's attitude made more sense to him.

"Nigga, I ain't stressin' it!" Phareed raised his voice. He felt that showing stress was a sign of weakness.

"Cool. I hear you." Stone put his hands up to calm him. Stone didn't want to escalate Phareed's anger. He had a short fuse, and when he went off it took awhile to get him back to normal.

"Holla at your boy and find out who this mother-fuckin' cowboy cop is. Tell him to get Lone Ranger off my ass."

"Bet. I'll holla at him. What this cop look like?"

"He'll know who I'm talkin' 'bout." Phareed's phone rang. "Yo," he answered.

He listened to the person on the other end with a scowl on his face.

"A'ight. I'm comin'." He hung up the phone. "I gotta bounce. Isis is trippin' on some shit down at the Trap. Come with."

"Nah. I'm gonna try and catch the end of the Sixers at home."

"Nigga, you a lame." Phareed smiled and shook his head.

Stone agreed. "I like my crib. What can I say? I worked hard to get mine, and I want to enjoy."

"I hear that." They slapped palms. All the tension that was between them before was gone. That's how it was between the two men. They were like brothers.

Phareed got into his truck while Stone went to open the metal door.

"Yo," Phareed called out from his truck as he pulled up next to Stone.

"'Sup?"

"Tomorrow night you comin' to the Pearl. I'm having some off-the-hook shit goin' down."

"Word." Stone smiled. He knew that when Phareed said "off the hook," he meant it. Tonight Stone would chill; tomorrow he would rage with Phareed.

Phareed smiled, then got serious and pointed at Stone. "Call your man. Fix this." Phareed drove off.

Stone got into his truck and made the call. When his man answered he said, "Meet tomorrow. The spot." He hung up the phone.

# Chapter 9

Billie held the napkin with Stone's number on it. She knew once she made this call there was no going back. The train would start rolling and would just keep on picking up speed. Was she ready? Hell, yes! She dialed the number.

Stone answered. "Stone."

"Hey. It's . . ." Her heart leapt into her throat. "Me."

*Fuck! I forgot the name I told him last week!*

"Who?" Stone asked.

*Shit.* "Me. You know, split lip from the bar."

"Oh, shit. Sheila! How you doin', ma? What took you so long?"

"I needed my face to heal a little before I could let you see me again."

"You were fine with a busted lip. You gonna be ridiculous all healed up."

"You too sweet." She smiled.

"I speak the truth. So what's up? We havin' our first date tonight?"

They were the exact words she was hoping to hear. "If you say so," she answered.

"I'll pick you up."

"Meet me at the Westin hotel. I'm staying there until I get my own place."

"I'll be there at ten."

"I'll be waiting." She hung up the phone happy. *One step closer to fucking up Phareed and his organization.*

Billie was waiting in the lobby of the Westin when Stone pulled up. She watched him step out of his Escalade and enter the hotel. He was better looking than she remembered. He was wearing a fitted, cream-colored button-down shirt, which showed off his muscular chest and arms. His perfectly pressed Armani jeans, expensive shoes, and Breitling watch told Billie that this nigga had money.

*Too bad this muthafucka is a thug. I might enjoy spending his money and rubbing up on that body,* she thought as he approached.

"Damn, you look fine." Stone gave her a kiss on the cheek.

Billie was wearing her favorite Gucci jeans, a sheer Calvin Klein blouse, and a pair of Prada heels. "Thanks. You not too bad yourself," she responded.

"Shall we?" She locked her arm inside his and led him right back out the door he'd just come through, wasting no time at all. She couldn't risk anyone recognizing her, especially if she was going to kill Stone tonight.

"Where are you taking me?" she asked as they drove through downtown Philadelphia.

"We headin' to a new club called Pearl. My man is having a big throw down tonight. Believe me, you don't want to miss his parties. Off the chain."

"That's what I'm talkin' about." She reached over and turned up the volume on the stereo. Stone smiled at Billie bobbing her head to the beat.

Stone pulled up in front of the club, and a valet came to the car immediately. He opened the door for Billie, then ran around to the driver's side door. Stone handed the valet his keys along with a fifty dollar bill.

"Thanks, Stone." The valet took the keys and money.

There was the usual line outside of Pearl waiting for the doorman to allow them entrance. Billie always thought it foolish to wait to be deemed good enough to be let in to a club.

"What up, Stone?" The doorman moved the red velvet rope to the side to allow Billie and Stone through. Stone had to clear a path to get to the front of the crowd and through the rope. Some of the people waiting started to gripe.

"What up, Curtis? This is Sheila," Stone said.

"Nice to meet you." Curtis shook Billie's hand.

"Phareed here?" asked Stone.

"Not yet."

Confetti started falling from the ceiling the second they stepped into the massive club. The dance floor was packed with people moving to the beats the DJ was spinning. There were girls dancing on stages surrounding the dance floor, and lasers were shooting off of every wall.

"You have anything like this in Pittsburgh?" Stone asked over the loud music.

"What?"

"Any clubs like this in Pittsburgh?" he asked

Luckily he thought she was asking for him to repeat because she didn't hear, but Billie had forgotten that she told him she was from Pittsburgh.

"Oh. Yeah. Nothing this big." *Shit, I need to step up my memory. Keep my lies in order,* she thought.

"Let's go." He grabbed her arm and pulled her through the dance floor. On the opposite side of the club they found the VIP section. Another red velvet rope was moved aside for them. This was where the real party was going to happen. This was where Billie was sure she would meet Phareed. She was stepping into the hornet's nest.

They walked up the six steps and into the private room overlooking the dance floor. The music was loud in the VIP room, but not as loud as the main club. It had just the right amount of people. There was room to walk, but it still felt crowded. The waitresses strutted by, carrying bottles to all the tables.

"You want a drink?" Stone asked.

"You know it. Vodka cran," she replied.

As Stone mixed her drink from the bottle on the table in front of them, Billie scanned the room. There seemed to be a mix of businessmen and men from Phareed's crew.

"You know everyone in here?" she asked as he handed her the drink.

"Most everyone. I do business with most of these guys."

"Wow. What do you do?" she asked.

"I'm an accountant." He bumped his glass against hers then took a sip. "Ugh." He squished his face in disgust. "I'm not much of a vodka man. I like my Heineken."

A waitress was walking by, and Stone gently grabbed her arm. "Can I get a Heineken?"

The waitress nodded and walked away. Billie chuckled as Stone put his glass on the table.

Stone wrapped his arm around Billie's waist. "Let's dance."

Billie took one last sip of her drink and placed it next to Stone's glass. They started dancing to the music and fell into perfect rhythm with each other. Stone was loving being out with this woman.

Billie was playing along while she scoped the club, waiting to see Phareed. She was now in work mode, and it was getting her energized. She loved this feeling of being on the hunt.

"Yo, Stone." Phareed had come up behind Billie.

Stone pulled away from Billie to greet Phareed. Billie turned and looked into the eyes of her target. His light brown eyes matched the tight Versace crew neck hugging his hulking muscles. His two-carat diamond stud earrings sparkled against his deep chocolate complexion.

"What's good?" Stone said.

"Damn? Who's this?" Phareed was looking at Billie.

"I'm Sheila." She put out her hand for him.

"We came together." Stone let Phareed know that she was off limits.

"A pleasure." Phareed looked seductively into Billie's eyes.

Isis cleared her throat. Billie's attention was diverted to Isis, who was standing behind Phareed and staring daggers at her.

"I'm Sheila." Billie introduced herself to Isis.

"Stay away from my man." Isis sucked her teeth and craned her neck as she looked Billie up and down.

"Isis, go get us a bottle of Moët," Phareed instructed.

She didn't dare say anything to Phareed for fear that he would get violent with her. She gave Billie one last stink eye before she sulked off in search of the champagne.

"Let's start this muthafuckin' party!" Phareed pulled out a vial of coke from his jeans.

He went and sat on one of the couches and proceeded to lay out three lines of the purest coke available in Philadelphia.

"Let's go, bitches," he said to Stone and Billie.

They both walked over to the couch. Stone sat down and started rubbing his palms together in anticipation. Billie remained standing. She didn't want to do any coke. She had her reputation as an ADA to think about; if she were ever caught with coke in her system she'd never be able to prosecute again. Plus, she had seen how even one hit could get people addicted, and end up ruining their lives. She'd seen it in the city, and she'd seen it in the courtroom. She'd always been afraid of trying the stuff. Of course, the immediate issue here was that she wanted to stay coherent and focused. She thought that if she started doing coke she might end up saying the wrong thing and getting found out. One slip-up could end her life a lot quicker than a coke addiction.

"I need to use the restroom," she blurted.

"Nah, girl. Sit down and do a hit first. Then go do your thing." Phareed moved over to make room for her next to him.

"I'm about to burst. I'll be back. Save me some." She winked at Phareed and walked toward the bathroom. Stone missed the wink because he was too busy snorting a line.

About halfway to the bathroom, Isis came stomping up to Billie and got right in her face. "I swear it, bitch. You stay the fuck away from my man."

"Excuse me?" Billie raised her eyebrows.

"I saw how you were lookin' at him like he was a well-aged steak. Don't even think about fuckin' him."

"Get out my face. I'll think about fuckin' whomever I damn well please. Now step."

"Bitch!" Isis started to go for Billie's throat. Billie easily swatted her hand away.

Before the fight could escalate, a huge bouncer came between the two ladies. "Is there a problem, ladies?"

"This bitch is after my man and she got all up in my face! Kick this heffa out!" Isis was pointing in Billie's face.

"Please, you got all up in my face with your insecure ass." Billie pursed her lips. She had grown up with plenty of girls like Isis and wasn't intimidated. She could stoop to their level and get just as ghetto if she needed.

"All right, both of you keep it movin'. If I see you at it again, you both out. Now go your separate ways."

"Gladly. I don't like to be this close to ghetto trash." Billie started walking toward the bathroom.

"Bitch!" Isis threw a flailing punch at the back of Billie's head and missed. The bouncer pushed Isis in the opposite direction away from Billie.

Billie entered the bathroom stall and locked it behind her. As soon as it was locked, she turned and leaned against the door and let out a huge breath. It was as if she was so excited to be near these men she was forgetting to breathe. Her adrenaline was sky high, especially after her run-in with Isis. She took a few more deep breaths to calm herself. She needed a clear plan on what to do next. But what was her plan? She couldn't really kill anyone tonight. It would be too obvious who did it. She needed to just chill tonight, gain their trust, and then attack later.

After talking herself through her plan, Billie freshened up in the mirror. Satisfied that she was looking good, she went back into the party.

As soon as she stepped out of the bathroom, Phareed grabbed her arm.

"Yo, holla at me." He pulled her into a corner. Phareed was using his muscular frame to trap her.

She seductively smiled at him. "Looks like I have no choice."

"I just want to get to know you, ma. When I see a fine piece, I want to know all about her."

"What you want to know?" She rested her hand on his bulging chest.

"You Stone's bitch?" he asked.

"I'm no one's bitch. I'm my own girl, free to do what I please." She rubbed his chest slowly as she looked directly in his eyes.

"A'ight." He shook his head. "You and me need some time alone. Know wha'mean?"

"I hear you loud and clear, daddy."

He pressed his hulking body closer to her. She gasped a little as she felt the weight pressing up against her.

"I got that ya-yo you wanted me to save." He pulled the vial out and poured a little on the back of his hand in the space between his thumb and forefinger.

Billie thought she had no choice this time. She had to do it if she was going to gain his trust and keep Phareed close. She leaned in, as slowly as she could, while her mind raced for another way out of this.

"That's it, baby," said Phareed. "You gonna enjoy this, ain't you?"

The lust in his voice gave her a brilliant flash of an idea. "Mmm," she said. "Actually, I see something I want to taste even more." She bypassed the coke entirely, traced her tongue down his forefinger, and inserted it in her mouth. She sucked and teased and nibbled it like a dick, and while she did that, she breathed hard enough out of her nose to blow the blow completely off Phareed's hand.

As she'd hoped, he forgot all about the coke as she worked his finger. "Oh shit, baby. We need to take this party somewhere else." Phareed moaned.

Billie did not want to leave the club with Phareed. To stall a little, she deep-throated his finger. Her lips hit his bottom knuckle as Phareed looked on with a huge smile on his face.

*This night is about to get freaky,* he thought.

*Pop! Pop! Pop! Pop!* Gunshots rang out in the club. The club turned to pandemonium as everyone panicked and started to take cover or run for the exits.

Billie released her suction on Phareed's finger.

"Shit." Phareed pulled out a nine from his waistband. "We gotta bounce."

*Pop! Pop! Pop!* More gunshots. It was now a shootout.

Billie and Phareed took off toward the exit. Billie got but about two feet before she got tackled. Phareed didn't see this and kept it moving. He disappeared into the crowd.

Billie was stunned for a second and then realized that Isis had tackled her.

"Bitch, I told you to stay away from Phareed." Isis started pulling Billie's hair. Each woman struggled to gain control of the other.

*Pop! Pop! Pop!*

Billie got an angle and punched Isis in her throat. Isis released Billie and grabbed her own throat as she gasped for air. Billie got up and started running for the door.

Billie got swallowed up by the crowd and pushed her way out the door. As soon as people made it outside, they scattered in all directions. It was chaos inside and outside of the club. Police cruisers with their lights flashing and their sirens blaring started screeching up to the club. Billie started running down the street, avoiding the police cruisers that were flying in from everywhere.

"Billie!" a voice called out from across the street.

Billie turned and saw Walter running toward her.

"Come with me!" He grabbed her and they started running in the direction that Walter had just come from. They both jumped in his car that was parked across from the club. Walter pulled away from the curb and sped down the street.

When they were far enough from the chaos, he slowed the car. "What were you doing there?" he asked.

"I was out with some girlfriends. I could ask you the same thing." Billie was going crazy on the inside. How long had he been there? What had he seen? She needed to find out what Walter knew.

"I was on a stakeout following a suspect. What happened in there?"

"Gunshots. Everyone started running. You weren't inside?"

"No. I was waiting outside. Been following this fool, waiting for him to slip up." Walter didn't want to tell her he was following Phareed because he was doing it for her and he was feeling a little self-conscious about that, especially since the other night at dinner hadn't ended well.

*Fuck. Did he see me show up with Stone?* "Who you following?" She was trying to remain calm and act normal. It wasn't easy—the gunshots, the fight, the running all had Billie's heart racing.

"I don't want to get into it," said Walter.

"You better tell me what you were doing there, Walter."

"Or else what?"

"Or else I'm gonna start thinking you were following me. That's it, isn't it? You were following me."

"Billie—"

"You just can't leave well enough alone, can you?"

"Billie!"

"I can't be smothered, Walter. You smother me, we're not going to see each other anymore. Oh, I'm sorry, actually you will see me . . . walking away from you."

"Billie, I was following Phareed."

Billie stopped in the middle of her rant. "You were?"

"Yes. I just don't want to fight anymore."

*Thank God,* Billie thought with such relief she almost said it out loud. *He got there after me.* Billie was grateful to her father or whoever else was looking out for her that she had arrived before Walter. He hadn't seen her arrive. This was too close of a call for her. She would need to be more careful from now on. "The force is starting an investigation?"

"We're always after this guy, but this is on my own."

"What?" She scrunched her face in confusion.

Walter kneaded the steering wheel. He didn't want to admit this part of the story to her, but as he looked over at her and saw once again how beautiful she was, he remembered how much he loved her. He couldn't help himself; he wanted to share everything with her, always. Finally, he broke down, sighed, and said,

"When I saw you after you got jumped, I couldn't handle it. I went to that corner and busted some heads, and this little shit started talking about Phareed this and Phareed that. That was it. I've had it. Phareed is responsible for hurting you, so I have made it my mission to arrest him, with or without the help of the force."

Even though Billie had more dire plans for Phareed, she was touched by Walter's valor. She would just have to get to him first and make sure that Walter never saw her.

She leaned over and kissed Walter on his cheek. "Let's go back to your place tonight."

He looked at her with a shocked expression. "You're not mad I'm going after him?"

"Why would I be?"

"You seemed like you just wanted all of this swept under the rug. Your attack and everything."

She shook her head. "How could I be mad at my knight in shining armor?"

As they pulled into Walter's driveway, a surge of excitement ran through Billie's body. In truth, her night at the club had her amped, and she needed to exert this energy and fuck Walter good. She could hardly make it to the door without grabbing Walter's manhood.

"Baby, you're ready, aren't you?" Walter said.

"Ready to get fucked," Billie replied.

"Oh, I'll fuck you all right, but first I'm going to lick that pussy real good."

Billie moaned at the thought of Walter's tongue circling her clit. She did not want to waste any time.

As they entered Walter's bedroom, he hoisted Billie on to her back and pulled down her jeans. As she lay there in her black leopard Hanky Panky thong, Walter took a minute to examine her body.

"With all the work that you do, baby, how do you have time to look this damn good? Mmm, I'm going to tear that shit up tonight," Walter said.

As he pulled off Billie's thong, he spread her legs and began devouring her pussy, moving his tongue up and down her lips. He licked her clit, and Billie gripped the sheets in ecstasy.

"Right there, baby. Just like that," Billie said. It felt so good she could hardly take it.

Just as she could feel her body tensing up for what she knew would be an earth-shattering orgasm, Walter quickly dropped his pants, jumped on top, and started pounding Billie with his hard cock.

"Fuck, Walter! Keep going. I'm going to cum!"

"Hold on, baby. I'm almost there with you," Walter replied.

"Grab my tits!" Billie shouted. "It's coming."

At this request, Walter was so turned on that he could hardly keep from squirting right then inside of Billie. He managed to keep fucking her hard with his monster dick as Billie let out a scream that could have woken the neighbors.

He could feel her love-hole tighten around his cock, and he quickly pulled out and came all over her tits.

"Holy fucking shit, baby. That was intense," Walter said.

"No shit. And so damn hot," Billie responded.

They lay there a minute in silence, catching their breath. Billie grabbed a Kleenex on the bedside table, wiped herself off, and turned on her side to face Walter.

She watched his chest rise and fall as he regained his normal breathing pattern. She felt a little sorry for this man who'd just had his way with her. He was a good man, and yet, there he was, lying beside a woman who killed the very men he wanted to put behind bars. If he only knew he just fucked the woman who chopped off a man's dick.

# Chapter 10

Billie crouched under her umbrella, shielding herself from the sideways rain as she ran into the archway entrance of the Widener building. The building was in downtown Philadelphia, where the main office of the district attorney was located.

She stood in the oversized entrance and shook out her umbrella, twisting it like a dog shaking its wet fur. She checked her phone for any messages in an attempt to stall the inevitable start of the workday. There were no messages.

Morphing into her "business bitch" mode, Billie confidently entered the building and headed for her office. She didn't really want to be in the office. In fact she hadn't really been in the office all that much since her last victory. Her priorities changed and she was more interested in her hunt than in sifting through legal documents. For the past few weeks, most days she would leave for an early lunch and just not return. Punishing criminals through the law seemed trivial to Billie at this point. She had her own form of justice that was much more satisfying.

As she walked down the carpeted hall, Kevin stuck his head out of his office. "Billie."

She rolled her eyes before turning around. She wasn't in the mood for his flirtations today.

"Yes, Kevin?" she said.

"Come here. I want to talk to you about something."

"Can it wait? I just got to work. I'd like to settle in." Listening to some of Kevin's bullshit first thing in the morning was not how Billie wanted to start the day.

"I think you'll want to hear this." He waved her toward his office.

Billie grudgingly entered his office, and Kevin closed the door behind her. She took a seat in one of the chairs across from his desk. His office was not very inviting. On his desk he had the typical picture of him holding up a large fish from a fishing trip, and one of him at an Eagles game. On the wall he had hung his diplomas and a mirror. A bookcase filled with legal books dominated the wall to Billie's left.

"So?" Billie said impatiently.

Kevin sat at his desk. "I've been looking for ways to go after Phareed, and I think I might have found one." He smiled.

*What the fuck?* Billie thought. "Since when have you been going after Phareed?" she asked with some agitation in her voice.

"A little while now. I'm looking to become mayor someday. If I initiate and win a high-profile case like Phareed's would be, my name would suddenly be thrown into the mix for mayor. At the very least for the next DA." Kevin seemed very pleased with himself.

Billie was infuriated that all of a sudden everyone around her seemed so hell-bent on catching Phareed.

He was her target. Everyone else needed to step back and let her operate.

"Sounds like you got big plans," she said evenly, trying to keep a calm exterior.

"I do, and I'm telling you this could be a huge break for me," he said excitedly.

Billie needed answers. "So what do you have on him? Something with those murders?"

She was not happy about this development. But if he was arrested at least she could take comfort in the fact that she had something to do with putting him away if he was tied to the murders. Even though death would be a better form of justice, maybe the organization would crumble if he was put away. At least that's what Billie had to tell herself in order to not fly off the handle and beat Kevin's ass.

"No. His taxes." Kevin said this like it was the most amazing revelation.

"What? Taxes?" Billie was disgusted.

"Yep." Kevin smugly leaned back in his chair.

"What kind of bullshit case are you going to bring with that? We need to get him on some real shit. You convict him on tax evasion charges and he may not even go to prison. Even if he does, he'll go to some country club minimum security." Billie was worked up.

"I don't care what kind of prison he goes to. At least we get him off the streets." Kevin was surprised by Billie's reaction.

"We need to bring serious justice down on his ass. He is ruining our city. He uses children to sell drugs in our communities. Who knows how many deaths he is responsible for? The man is a monster."

"Yes, that's why I'm going after him." Kevin was getting annoyed. "Look, you don't think he's prepared in case charges are brought against him for drugs, or even those murders? Do you know how many fall guys are lined up in case that happens? He won't see tax evasion coming, and if that's the only way I can get this guy, then so be it."

But Billie wasn't listening to his brand of logic. "We need to get him on more serious charges or it isn't worth it," she said, digging in her heels.

"Well, I'm going after him on whatever charges I can. Then next stop, City Hall," Kevin said with finality to his tone.

"Good luck with that." Billie couldn't stand to be in the room any longer. She felt like leaping over the desk and strangling Kevin. His pursuit of Phareed could seriously interfere with her plans. Kevin didn't care about justice; all he cared about was advancing his career.

Billie stomped back down the hall to her own office. She slammed her door behind her, and yanked her chair away from her desk to sit down. She threw herself down in it, and spun it around toward the window so she could look out at the lightning flashes and the pouring rain. Her mood matched the weather: angry.

It seemed that all of a sudden she had competition in the pursuit of Phareed, and if anyone else got to him first, she would not be happy. She was only going to gain satisfaction if she was able to get to him and kill him. She needed to spend all of her time infiltrating his crew and gaining his trust. Work hadn't been a priority for her recently, and now it was going to be even less so.

Billie grabbed her cell phone to call Stone, but before she was able to make the call, her office phone rang. She hesitated for a second to decide whether to answer it or let it go to voice mail.

"This is Billie," she answered.

"Billie, can you come to my office?" It was her boss.

"Now?"

"Yes, now." He sounded exasperated.

"Okay." She hung up.

"Damn. I knew I shouldn't have answered," she said as she got up from her desk.

On her way down to the DA's office, Billie took a few deep breaths, and pulled herself together. She pasted a cordial smile on her face before entering his main office, and then greeted the portly secretary guarding DA Lewis's inner office. "Hello, Diane."

"Hello, Billie. He's waiting." She raised her eyebrows and motioned toward his door.

"Thanks." Billie headed for the thick oak door.

"Good luck."

Billie turned her head to the secretary and rolled her eyes.

The secretary just smiled and shook her head at the confidence Billie always exuded.

When Billie entered the office, Stanley Lewis leaned back in his soft leather chair. "Come in, Billie."

She sat in the cream-colored velvet chair opposite her boss. It was a chair she had sat in many times before, mostly following another court victory or to strategize about how to take down the next criminal on their list.

"How are you?" he asked.

"I'm fine," she said nonchalantly.

"Do you know why I called you in here?"

Billie couldn't help thinking that her boss sounded like a junior high principal about to scold a student. She found the question demeaning.

"If I could read minds, I wouldn't be working for the low pay I get here."

He wasn't amused by her answer or her tone. "Billie, what's going on with you?"

"Nothing." She didn't want to get into some personal conversation with her boss. They weren't friends, and they never would be.

"Okay, look. Your work has obviously been lacking lately. I expect a lot from you, and what you have been producing lately, which has been nothing, isn't cutting it. So what is going on?"

The last thing Billie wanted to do was answer his stupid question, but she wanted this conversation to be as short as possible. "I'm having some private, personal issues that I don't want to discuss at the moment."

Stanley shook his head in concerned agreement. "I understand. If you need to talk about it, my door is always open."

Again, Billie couldn't help but think of junior high school. She almost laughed in Stanley's face at his attempt to bond with her.

She controlled her laugh and answered, "Thank you."

"With that being said, if you are working, you need to put those issues to the side and focus. I have big ambitions for you, and I don't want this dip in production to affect any of that."

"You're right." She wanted to appease him and get the hell out.

"I'm glad we agree. Now, I want you to assist Kevin on the Mendez case."

"Wouldn't you rather I help him compile the case against Phareed and his crew?"

"We aren't going after Phareed." He had a curious look on his face.

"We're not?" asked Billie, before she realized that when Kevin had said he was initiating a case against Phareed, he really meant it.

"What gave you that idea?"

Billie waved it off. "I guess I was mistaken." She realized that her boss had no idea that Kevin was going after Phareed. Billie could see the wheels turning in her boss's head. This was the first he had heard anything about this. Billie was pleased that she had let the cat out of the bag. Maybe her boss would stop Kevin from investigating.

"Yes, you must be. Anyway, we are about to get Mendez to cop to a plea."

"Didn't they catch Mendez with thirty-five grams of heroin and a gun implicated in a murder?" Billie was taken aback that they would even consider bargaining with him.

"Yes, they know our case is a slam dunk, so they are about to plead guilty to get fifteen years," he said proudly.

"That's bullshit." She raised her voice. "You should be going after him with the max sentence."

"Relax. We're winning the case and putting him away for a long time."

"Not long enough. Everyone is so damn complacent in this office." Her voice trailed off as she shook her head in frustration.

"Sometimes we have to make sacrifices. Did I ever tell you about my first year in the DA's office? I was handed this major case—"

"I'm done." Billie had had enough. She stopped her boss from telling one of his boringly endless stories about the good old days. She was through with playing by the rules.

"Excuse me?" Stanley was a little offended at being cut off.

"I need to take a leave of absence. I have some vacation days and personal days that I want to use, and then I want to officially be on a leave of absence," she said matter-of-factly.

"Billie, think about this. Are you sure?"

"I've never been more sure of anything." She stood from her chair. Before she exited, she turned to her boss with one final parting shot. "It's not me you should be worried about going after your job. You've got another shark circling your office." With that she walked out of the office ready to hunt her prey.

She got back to her office and was gathering her things when Kevin popped his head into her office. "What happened?"

"What do you mean? Nothing happened." She picked up her purse.

"What did the boss say?"

"He said nothing. I'm taking some time off."

"Did he suspend you?" Kevin asked.

"Stop being such a gossiping little girl." She brushed past him, then stopped and turned. "By the way, the boss knows you are trying to build a case against Phareed behind his back."

Kevin's face went red with a look of panic. Billie got the reaction she wanted then proceeded to the exit.

# Chapter 11

"What the fuck happened last night?" Stone passed the blunt to Phareed. They were in Phareed's Hummer, driving to the Honey Trap.

"Them niggas Seven-up and Germ started beefing. You know Germ. That nigga start poppin' off instantaneous."

"Those niggas need to control theyselves."

"What happened to you?" Phareed asked.

"I got the fuck out. Got swept up in the crowd and surfed that shit right out the door. You know I ain't waitin' around for no cops."

"Word." Phareed took a hit off the blunt. "Yo, what happened with ya girl last night?"

"I lost her in the melee." He took the blunt from Phareed.

Stone's phone vibrated in his pocket. He took it out and looked at the caller ID. The number came up blocked. He contemplated whether to answer, then decided to hear who it was. "Stone."

"Hey, baby. What happened to you last night? You okay?" Billie purred into the phone.

He was happy he decided to answer. "Oh, shit. Speak of the devil. I was just talkin' about you with Phareed."

"Only nice things, I hope," she flirted.

"Always. What you doin', ma?"

"Waitin' to see you again."

"I got some business to attend to, but let me holla at you later," he said.

"I like the sound of that. Text me the address."

"Bet." Stone smiled.

"See you tonight, daddy." Billie hung up.

"Yo, that girl got my dick twitchin'," Stone said to Phareed.

"I hear that. That bitch got a slammin' body."

Stone didn't like Phareed talking about Billie like that, but he couldn't say anything. He hadn't fucked Billie, so he couldn't lay any claim to that ass just yet.

"Word." Stone stared out the passenger window, enjoying his high.

Phareed pulled up in front of the Honey Trap. "Make sure your man know he need to take care of the thorn in our side."

"You not comin' in?" Stone asked.

"Nah. I got to talk to them niggas Seven-up and Germ. Make sure they know if they get pinched, my name never comes out they mouth. They should be plannin' on leavin' this city for a minute. Hear me?"

"I hear that. I'll take care of this thing."

They gave each other a pound and Stone hopped out of the Hummer. Before he entered the club he texted the address to Billie.

She replied with a winking smiley face.

Stone entered the dark club. It was the usual early evening crowd, a few guys sitting around the stage watching the girls dance. The energy was low in the main room. The guys were tired from working all day, and the girls on the afternoon shift were never too excited to be there.

Stone ordered a beer from the bartender. He leaned against the bar and watched the girls gyrating for cash. One or two girls were lucky enough to convince some of the guys to get a lap dance, which meant more money in their pockets. Stone's high was kicking in lovely at this point. He finished his beer then went into the office to wait for his man to show up.

Stone was sitting at his desk, going through some paperwork, when his man came into the office.

"I've got to make this quick."

"Then let's get right to it," Stone said. "Some cop got in Phareed's face. We need it taken care of."

"Goddamn. I knew it."

Stone gave him a questioning look.

"That cop is my partner," D'Angelo responded to his look. He squeezed his face tight. He knew he would regret the day he agreed to do some favors for Stone.

D'Angelo had known Stone since childhood. They weren't the closest friends growing up but they did know each other from around the way. While he was still in the police academy D'Angelo's mother had gotten sick and he needed some cash. Stone was there to help him out but in return he wanted D'Angelo to do him some favors. D'Angelo was hesitant at first but Stone assured him that the favors would be easy. He thought it over but ultimately decided to take the money and pay his mother's hospital bills. Stone didn't ask for the favors right away; he waited until D'Angelo made it on to the police force to cash them in.

Stone didn't lie to D'Angelo, they were simple favors. He mostly had D'Angelo busting rival corner boys and disrupting their business so Phareed and Stone could move in. A few times he had him plant evidence on people or fix some paperwork so one of Phareed's crew could get off.

D'Angelo started getting invited to parties by Stone. He also started accepting extra cash from Stone, which afforded D'Angelo a lifestyle he thought he would never be able to afford. Over time D'Angelo began to enjoy these perks a little too much. He became too comfortable around Phareed's crew and soon Stone saw an opportunity to blackmail D'Angelo and he took it.

One night at a party Stone had one of their hoes get close to D'Angelo and convince him to do some blow with her. What D'Angelo didn't know was that Stone was videotaping the entire thing. By the end of the night Stone had hours of video of D'Angelo and a prostitute blowing lines and fucking each other.

Stone approached him with an offer. He proposed that D'Angelo keep working for them and make extra cash, or say no and take his chances in court when the videotape was leaked to the media. D'Angelo was stuck. He had to keep working for Phareed no matter how much risk he was taking within the force.

"Damn." Stone shook his head slowly. He knew D'Angelo had a new partner, but he wasn't expecting it to be this pest. "Why the fuck you let him do this?" Stone asked.

"I tried to stop him. He wasn't listening to any of it." D'Angelo shrugged. He knew this was going to come back on him.

"Well, fuck, you need to make him listen and get the fuck off our ass."

"I'll see what I can do." He was annoyed that he didn't try harder to nip it in the bud sooner.

"See what you can do? Nigga, you gon' make sure this shit goes away. That's what you can do," Stone threatened.

"This isn't going to be easy. He is going full force after Phareed."

"If you can't talk him down or sabotage his ass, then you know what needs to be done." Stone went to the safe under the desk. He twirled the dial on the door and unlatched the lock. He reached in and pulled out a stack of bills, then handed it to D'Angelo. "Listen, nigga, just make it go away."

"Shit." D'Angelo gritted his teeth and took the money.

There was a knock on the door as D'Angelo stuffed the money into the inside pocket of his coat. He placed his hand on the pistol that was sitting in its holster. Stone and D'Angelo gave each other a look that said, "who the fuck is that?"

"I'm going out the back," D'Angelo said quietly.

Stone shook his head in acknowledgment. He rested his hand on the gun in his waistband. Using the door as a shield, he kept it between his body and the person on the other side. He poked his head around the corner. "Oh, shit. What are you doing here?"

"You told me to come," Billie said.

D'Angelo looked back just before he closed the door, and he saw Billie entering the office. D'Angelo had no idea that he was looking at his partner's girl. Since Walter and D'Angelo had only been working together for a short time they still hadn't gone out together with their girls. D'Angelo just figured that Billie was some girl coming in looking for a job. The sound of the closing door caught Billie's attention.

"I didn't think you were going to be here this soon," Stone said.

"I couldn't wait to see you. Was someone else in here?" She pointed to the door.

"Business partner. He just left."

"Oh. So you do your business in a strip club?" She said with a hint of flirtation.

"This is just one of my businesses."

"Right, you own a bar." She pressed her body against his.

"That's right." He palmed her ass.

"What are we doing tonight?" She rubbed her hands down his back and palmed his ass.

"Whatever you want, ma." He smiled.

"Mmmm. I like that. Let's get out of here."

They broke their embrace. Stone went to close the safe, but before he did he took out $20,000 in cash and put it in his pocket. He was going to make sure they had fun.

As they walked through the club, Isis was dancing onstage. She was bent over in some guy's face, taking a dollar from him. She saw Stone and Billie leaving together and gave Billie a look that could kill. Billie just gave her a shit-eating grin and kept it moving.

They got in Stone's Escalade and drove off.

"Where we going?" Billie asked.

"You'll see." Stone pulled onto I-76 headed north.

About twenty-five minutes later, they were pulling into the King of Prussia Mall parking lot.

"You like shopping?" Stone asked.

"Yes," Billie said hesitantly.

"Get ready, 'cause we gonna blow it out up in here." Stone pulled into a parking space. They got out and walked across the parking lot arm in arm. Billie would rather be getting closer to Phareed but if Stone wanted to go shopping she had to play along. He was her ticket to Phareed at this point. If he wanted to buy her clothes that was his choice, and Billie definitely wasn't going to stop him from doing that.

"Let the shopping spree begin." Stone opened the door for Billie.

They spent the next three hours shopping. They went to all the department stores and the most expensive boutiques. At the end of it all, Stone had dropped fifteen grand easy on clothes.

"Let's eat. I'm hungry," Stone said, his arms full of shopping bags.

"The food court?" she suggested.

"Hell no. We gonna eat right tonight."

They drove back to Philly and went to Smith & Wollensky's steakhouse. He ordered a prime rib, and she ordered the porterhouse. They dined on appetizers and drank a couple bottles of the best wine they offered.

They laughed and flirted throughout the meal. The wine, the food, the atmosphere of the restaurant all had Billie feeling completely at ease with Stone. They had the same tastes in music, movies, and TV. Stone was making her laugh by doing impressions of famous people. He was so good that Billie thought he could be doing it on stage.

After paying the $1,200 bill, Stone helped a tipsy Billie out to the car. As soon as the fresh air hit Billie, she was snapped back to reality. She wasn't on a real date; she was hunting and needed to focus.

"We goin' back to my place?" Stone asked as they got back in the Escalade.

Billie looked at him with a coy smile on her face. "I'm not so sure about that."

"What you talkin' about? We had fun tonight."

"Yes, we did."

"So let's keep it goin'. Let me take you back to my crib and sex you like you deserve." He put his hand on her thigh.

"Mmmmm. That sounds good, but I like you. I want to take it slow with you."

"If you like me, that's all the more reason to come back with me."

"I want to, but I can't. I'm embarrassed to say this, but I'm on my period." She gave him a disappointed frown.

"That's cool. I don't care about that."

She could see that he wasn't going to take no for an answer. Even though she wasn't exclusively dating Walter, she still felt that sleeping with someone else would be cheating. In her head, she was desperately searching for a way out.

"I care. It's gross," she said.

"Come on." He was almost pleading at this point.

Billie weighed her options. She couldn't kill him yet, because people had seen them at dinner. She saw only one way out. She told herself it wasn't cheating.

"How 'bout I suck your dick, daddy?" She leaned over and started undoing his pants.

Stone had a huge smile on his face as he watched her unzip his fly and release his rock-hard nine inches.

She started kissing the tip. "Mmmm, tasty." She inserted his dick into her mouth.

Stone looked on as she bobbed up and down on his dick. He grabbed the back of her head and started pushing it down.

"Yeah, let me fuck your face," he said.

His dick was covered in her saliva as she took his entire shaft all the way to the base. Stone could feel his dick hitting the back of her throat. This sensation put him over the edge. He accelerated his thrusts and gripped her hair tighter. She cupped his balls and kept up with his rhythm. With one last thrust, he kept his dick down her throat and released his load. She swallowed it all. She didn't let one drop out of her mouth.

She came up from his lap, wiping her mouth and chin of the excess saliva. "Mmmmm," she moaned.

"Damn, you got some head game, ma." He was catching his breath and putting his dick back in his pants.

"When I have such a nice piece of meat to work with, it's easy." She smiled and sat back in her seat secretly disgusted by what she just had to do.

"Where to?" Stone started his truck.

"Take me to the Westin."

"We got to find you a crib." He pulled into the street.

"I'm workin' on it."

When they got to the hotel, Billie exited the Escalade and started walking toward the entrance to the Westin.

"Sheila!" Stone called from his truck.

She turned. She had forgotten the name she had given to Stone once; she would never forget it again.

"Your clothes."

"I'll get them from you next time," she called back and waved.

"A'ight." He pulled off.

She watched him turn the corner, waited a minute to make sure he wouldn't return for any reason, and then she called a cab to take her home.

On the cab ride home, Billie reflected on her night. She was confused. There was a part of the night when she was genuinely enjoying herself. She wasn't acting. Was it the alcohol? She didn't know, but in order for her to stay on task, she needed to blame it on the alcohol.

# Chapter 12

The next morning Billie woke to her ringing phone. Her headache reminded her of all the wine she had consumed the previous night. Her cottonmouth was telling her to ignore the phone and get a glass of water.

"Hello." Her voice sounded like she had swallowed razor blades.

"Did I wake you?" Walter asked.

"Yes." She cleared her throat as she grudgingly got out of bed and poured a glass of water from the bottle she kept on her nightstand.

"Billie, what's going on? You quit your job?" He sounded concerned.

Billie thirstily gulped the entire glass of water. "I didn't quit. I took a leave of absence."

"Why?"

"I just need some time to myself." She went for the bottle again to pour herself another glass.

"Well, let me see you tonight. I want to talk about this."

Billie hesitated, the water bottle in her hand, but she figured she was going to have to talk to him about it sooner or later. *Might as well make it sooner.*

"What time?" She continued pouring.

"I'll pick you up at eight."

"All right. See you then." She hung up and drank her second glass of water.

She started to prepare herself some breakfast, then decided there was no reason for her to stay up. She stopped what she was doing and went back to bed to sleep off her wine headache.

She woke around noon feeling much better. Now instead of a headache she had a growling stomach screaming for food. Billie entered her kitchen and finished the breakfast she had started preparing earlier. Some fresh fruit, yogurt, and whole wheat toast satisfied her grumpy stomach.

Billie sat at her kitchen table, sipping her tea while she read the local newspaper. She almost spit her tea out when she saw the article on page six. It told the story of the discovery of a body along the river. It said that it appeared to be a murder and there were definite signs of a struggle. It said police were investigating many possibilities, including one that it could have been a clandestine sex meeting gone wrong. Billie figured they might have thought that because his pants were down when she killed him. She read the article a second time looking for signs that she might be a suspect. Still not comfortable after reading it again, she called Walter to see if she could pump him for information.

"Hey. What's up?" he answered.

"Nothing. Just wondering what we are doing tonight so I know what to wear."

"Figured we could go to Tessie's."

"Good. Casual. Hey, I read an article about that body found along the river. You assigned that case?"

"No, pretty gruesome though."

"Yeah. What are they thinking happened?"

"Probably some gay hookup gone bad. Anyway, I gotta go. I'm investigating two other murders. Get this, it's the same two guys suspected of shooting up that nightclub the other night. I'll see you at eight."

"See you." She hung up. Billie was relieved to know she wasn't a suspect at this time.


Billie was putting the finishing touches on her makeup when Walter rang her bell. She quickly applied the rest of her lipstick then went and answered the door. The second she opened the door and saw Walter's face a flashback of her sucking Stone's dick crossed her mind. She instantly felt guilty. She may have convinced herself the night before that it wasn't cheating but at the moment she knew she cheated.

"Hey." She smiled awkwardly.

"You ready?" he said.

"Let me get my purse."

The energy in the car ride to Tessie's felt strained. They both knew that they were going to talk about Billie's leave of absence but neither one brought it up. Instead they talked about the weather and what they might want to eat at the restaurant.

They arrived at Tessie's exactly on time for their reservation and were seated immediately. Walter ordered a bottle of wine, which Billie wasn't in the mood for. Just the thought of drinking wine made Billie's head thump but she couldn't tell Walter. So she played along and let him pour her a glass. Another flashback of Stone cumming in her mouth and another pang of guilt swept over Billie. She hoped this guilt would pass over time.

"So, what happened? Why are you taking a leave of absence?"

"I'm getting burnt out. I've been working way too much. I was going to crack if I didn't get away from there." She had been rehearsing this answer all day.

"Why didn't you talk to me about this?"

"It's my problem, not yours. I can deal with it."

"I want to help you deal with it."

"Stop it," she warned.

"What? Billie, I care about you."

"I know. You tell me all the time. I'm going through some things." Her voice started to get louder but, try as she might, it seemed she couldn't lower it. "I can deal with it. I'll be fine. Can we just sit here and enjoy our meal and not have to talk about how you always want to help?"

Walter was stunned and hurt. He now had a decision to make: break it off with her, or give her the space she wanted and trust that everything would work out.

Billie got her wish: they did just sit there while they waited for their food to arrive, which seemed to take forever. A few times Walter looked as though he wanted to say something, even getting as far as opening his mouth. But then he'd cover with a cough, or by clearing his throat, and he wouldn't say a word.

A part of her felt bad about causing him so much grief. She knew he just cared about her. But she couldn't think about him or his motives right now. Her headache was coming back with a vengeance. All she wanted to do was get through this dinner, have some food on her stomach, and get back home again.

Finally, Walter seemed to find his voice. "I'm sorry if I'm smothering, but I care. If you need me to back off, fine. I will. Let's just enjoy tonight." He raised his wine glass, and Billie did the same. They tapped them together in salutation just as the food arrived. They had both ordered Tessie's famous burgers.

Walter started in on his burger right away so he wouldn't keep talking about Billie's situation. He acted like he was fine with what was happening with their relationship, but he was hurting.

Billie took her knife and cut her burger in half. She couldn't stop comparing this night with the previous night. *Steaks last night, hamburgers tonight*, she thought. She was having trouble looking Walter in the eye. Billie was certain that Walter was picking up on her awkwardness.

"So who were you at the club with the other night?" Walter asked between bites.

"Some girlfriends."

"I know. Who?"

"What does it matter? You don't know them. Why do you want to be so involved with my life?" Billie's voice was rising along with her anger from the guilt she was feeling.

"It's just a question. Calm down."

"You know what? Take me home. I'm not feeling well." She got up from the table.

"Billie . . ." Walter threw down some cash for the bill and followed Billie out the door.

It was windy tonight. Her hair whipped around her face, and the chilly breeze made Billie shudder and hug herself. She tried not to pay any attention to the elements as she stormed away.

"Billie. Where are you going?" he called out to her across the parking lot.

"Home." She kept walking.

Walter quickly got in his car and drove up next to her as she continued to walk. "Get in. I'll give you a ride."

She kept walking and didn't say anything.

"Don't be stubborn. What are you going to do, walk home?" He drove slowly next to her.

She walked a few more feet, then stopped. She stood there for a second, staring straight ahead. She so badly wanted to ignore him, but now the wind was making her eyes water and biting at her skin. She heaved a sigh, and then opened the passenger door and got in.

Neither one said a thing during the ride back to Billie's house. Walter was feeling rejected. Billie was embarrassed at the way she was acting.

Walter pulled in front of Billie's house. "Here you go," he said.

Billie looked at Walter, feeling bad. "I'm sorry. I just need time to figure things out." She got out of the car and walked into her house.

Walter watched with a heavy heart until she got inside. He put the car in drive and headed for home, unaware of the car that had been following him all night.

# Chapter 13

D'Angelo called Stone. He had just gotten a good look at the woman who was with Walter as they walked into Tessie's restaurant.

Stone's phone went directly to voice mail. "Yo, it's me. Call me as soon as you get this," D'Angelo said after the beep.

D'Angelo needed to hear from Stone. He needed to know the story of this girl. Was she working with Stone, or was she working with Walter? He knew she wasn't a prostitute because Walter had picked her up from her house, but she was definitely working with someone.

Every few minutes he would check his phone to make sure he hadn't missed any calls; then he would call Stone again. Each call yielded the same results: no ring, directly to voice mail. D'Angelo couldn't believe that Stone would have his cell phone off. He was frustrated. He wasn't about to leave any information on voice mail, so he didn't leave any message after his first.

D'Angelo perked up in his car seat when he saw the woman come charging out of Tessie's. He was surprised she was without Walter. Then Walter came chasing after her a few seconds later. D'Angelo could hear Walter call out to her. The name Walter used was different from the name Stone called her. Now D'Angelo was thoroughly confused and suspicious. He slouched down in his car seat to make sure he wasn't spotted. He watched the scene unfold in front of him. Walter got in his car and drove next to Billie, trying to convince her to get in. He watched as she ignored him for a few moments, but then got in.

D'Angelo started his car and followed them. He made sure to stay far enough behind to avoid detection.

After following them for a while, he watched them pull up in front of Billie's house. D'Angelo parked down the block and watched as Billie walked into her house and Walter drove off. D'Angelo decided to follow Walter and see what his next move would be. The entire time he followed Walter, he couldn't stop thinking about Billie. Who was this woman, and how did she fit into this whole thing? He ran through several scenarios in his head about why she would be meeting with both Stone and Walter and giving two different names, but he couldn't come to any definitive conclusions.

As soon as D'Angelo realized Walter was heading back to his home he cancelled his trail. He was much more intrigued by this woman, and he was going to get to the bottom of who she was.

D'Angelo turned his car around and headed straight back to Billie's house. He pulled in front and cut his engine, then stayed in his car for several minutes planning his next move. He reached in the glove box, took out a pair of leather gloves, and slid them on. He flexed his fingers in and out of a fist to loosen the snug leather.

He walked up to the front door and rang the bell. When he heard Billie's footsteps walking to the door, his heart rate picked up.

Billie opened the door, still dressed in the same clothes from her evening out. "Walter, I'm . . ." She stopped in mid-sentence when she saw it wasn't Walter.

"I'm sorry. I thought you were someone else." She could sense that something was not right, and got that uneasy feeling in her stomach.

He slammed his hands into her chest, pushing her back into her house. Then he quickly stepped in and closed the door behind him.

Billie recovered her balance and moved away from him to create more distance between them.

"Who are you?" D'Angelo asked.

"Stay away from me. I'll have you arrested." She kept slowly backing away.

"Who are you?" He moved toward her slowly.

"I'm fucking warning you."

"Billie or Sheila?" he asked.

Billie's eyes widened at the question, which caught her off-guard. She had been found out, and this guy was here to kill her. "Who are you?" she asked.

"I'm an associate of Phareed."

"Then you should know who I am. Ask Phareed."

Billie needed to stall and figure a way out of this. She had to keep this guy talking, then attack.

"Believe me, I will. But why don't you clarify with me who the fuck you are?"

"Phareed won't be happy if you kill me."

"I'm not gonna kill you. Yet. Let's take a ride and see Phareed and Stone. See what they have to say about you and your two names." He rushed at her.

She tried to run away, but he easily caught her and tackled her. She struggled to get free, but before she could do anything, he had her hands in zip ties. He pulled her up by her bound wrists and pushed her out the door. She tried putting up a fight, but with her hands behind her back it was useless. D'Angelo shoved her into the front seat of his car. While he was trying to buckle her seat belt, she bit into his neck. He pulled away and grabbed her by the throat and squeezed.

"I will fucking end you, bitch."

Billie fought to take a breath, but her airway was shut. She kicked her legs and writhed around in an attempt to free herself, but D'Angelo's grip was too tight. After a few seconds of torture, D'Angelo released his grip. Billie took a huge breath, filling her lungs with oxygen. She could feel her windpipe throbbing.

D'Angelo drove them to the rear entrance of the Honey Trap. He pulled her down the short hallway and pushed her into Phareed's office. Billie was relieved to see the office empty. She still had time to find a way out of this.

"Where the fuck are these two?" D'Angelo said. He locked the door behind them. "Don't fucking move. I'm going to find them." He exited the door that led to the main part of the club.

Billie frantically searched the room for anything that might be used to cut her wrists free. There was nothing out in the open, so she moved her search to the desk. She backed up to the desk, grabbed a hold of a handle, and opened a drawer. It was empty. She rummaged through the next one but didn't feel anything but papers. The third drawer was filled with junk—pencils, pens, paper clips, old cell phones. She was starting to lose hope that she would find anything. She figured if they had anything for her to use it would have been in this drawer. She pushed her fears to the side and continued her search.

The final drawer was a lower drawer that she had to sit on the floor to open. She sat down and scooted herself against the desk, grabbed the handle, and opened the drawer. She blindly reached in and felt around. Empty.

"Shit!"

She sat for a second trying to calm her mind and gather her thoughts. It was useless. She was in panic mode. Reopening the junk drawer, she started to search again. Maybe she could figure out a way to use a pen or something. When she turned to see what was in the drawer, she couldn't believe her eyes. There was a pair of scissors toward the back. *How did I not feel those before?*

She spun back around and reached for the scissors, straining to get her hands far enough back to grab on to them. She had to torque her shoulders so much she felt like she was going to dislocate them. Not being able to see what she was doing wasn't making it any easier. She was finally able to get a hold of the handle with one of her fingers and slide it closer to her. Once the scissors were closer, she was able to grab them and take them out.

Billie was quickly trying to maneuver the scissors in her hand to cut her wrists free. She was having trouble positioning them to get the ties between the blades. She finally got them into position and was about to squeeze the handle when the scissors slipped from her grasp and fell to the floor.

"Shit."

She immediately got on the floor and went for the scissors. It was easier for her this time to get them in her hands. She began to get the blades in position.

The door opened. "Where the fuck are you?" D'Angelo called out.

Billie was on the floor behind the desk, shielded from his sight.

She stayed quiet but continued to maneuver the blades. She could hear him coming toward her as she struggled to get the blades in position.

D'Angelo appeared at the corner of the desk. "What the fuck you doin' down there?"

"I fell." Billie had the blades in position to free her wrists.

"Well, get the fuck up."

"I can't."

Just as D'Angelo started toward her, she cut the zip tie then lunged forward, stabbing him in the stomach.

"Aggghhhhh! Fuck!" He hunched over and grabbed for her wrist. She was too quick and was able to pull the scissors out before he could get control of them. D'Angelo covered the puncture wound with his hand

and went after Billie. As soon as he made a move, she plunged the scissors deep into his chest, puncturing his heart. This stopped him cold. He froze for a second with a stunned look on his face. Out of instinct, he moved his hand from his stomach to his heart. He stood there and swayed back and forth just staring at Billie. She didn't know if he was in shock or what.

Billie's adrenaline was up, her hands were bloody, and her breathing was rapid. She was like a wild dog.

D'Angelo took a step toward Billie, and she unleashed her fury on him. She started stabbing him over and over and over. By the time she stopped, she had stabbed him a total of thirty-seven times and his mutilated body lay on the floor in a pool of blood.

Billie collapsed to her knees in exhaustion, unsure if she wanted to scream or cry. As she stared at the lifeless body in front of her, the office door opened.

Billie's head snapped in the direction of the door to see who it was. "Oh my God, Phareed."

"What the fuck?" He stood in the doorway.

Billie got up from the floor and slowly started toward him, forcing tears to well up in her eyes. "Phareed, he . . . he tried to rape me," she said between sobs.

When Billie got close enough to Phareed, he slapped her across the face. "The fuck you thinkin', bitch?"

She was stunned. "I had to defend myself." She held her stinging face.

"No, you didn't. If a nigga wants to have sex, just do it. The fuck is wrong with you? What are you even doin' here?" He shoved Billie by her shoulders. She went flying back and almost fell onto D'Angelo's body.

"I came to see you; then he attacked me." She was coming up with her story on the fly. Lying had become so much easier for her lately.

"I don't give a fuck. You murked a cop, you dumb bitch."

Billie's heart sank instantly. The blood rushed from her face, and she felt like she was going to pass out.

"Yeah, that's right. He was a fuckin' cop." Phareed saw the look of terror in her eyes.

"Oh, fuck," she said, barely above a whisper. "What are we gonna do?"

"You done enough already. You ain't gonna do shit. I'ma take care of this and you gonna owe my ass."

"Anything you want," she said.

He smiled devilishly. "Damn right."

He looked at the body as he paced around it, making sure to avoid stepping in the blood. He got on his phone and made a call.

"Jumbo, I need you to clean up a mess at the office." He listened to Jumbo's response. "I'll be here." He hung up the phone.

"This is gonna cost you. You gonna have to earn me some money."

"How?"

"Well, since it seems niggas want to get at that pussy, I'ma put you in my stable of bitches."

Billie hesitated before speaking. "You want me to be a prostitute."

"I prefer my women to be called escorts, but yeah, you gonna be a fuckin' whore and pay me back for killin' a cop in my office."

Billie started trying to think of a way out of this, and then she realized she might be in a good position. This could be her chance to kill Phareed. No one saw them come in, and the only one who had seen her in the office was dead. But the question was, how would she do it? The only way she saw to kill him was with the scissors. She had to get those scissors.

"Okay, I can do that," she said, stalling for time as she tried to formulate her plan of attack. "As long as I get a cut from my tricks." She tried to see the scissors out of the corner of her eye without Phareed noticing. This was going to have to happen fast.

"Oh shit, a little businesswoman on my hands. Before we discuss any of that, you know I gots to sample my product."

"You sayin' you wanna fuck?" She sexily narrowed her eyes and puckered her lips. He stepped toward Billie. This was her chance. She was going to make a move for the scissors.

She got a surge of energy at the thought of finally killing Phareed. One more step and she would go for the scissors.

Billie felt like she was watching in slow motion as Phareed went to take his final step. Just as his foot landed, she leaped for the scissors. At that exact moment, Jumbo came into the office. Luckily, Billie was able to make her sudden movement look like she was just startled by the door opening, so Phareed didn't suspect her real motives. Unfortunately, there were now two people she would have to kill. She knew her odds against two of them were not good.

"Oh shit." Jumbo was looking at the gruesome scene.

"Wait out in the club," Phareed said to Billie.

"Okay." She left the office and went into the main room of the strip club. She sat at a table and watched as Isis was again dancing on the stage. Isis saw her and started mean mugging her. Billie found it humorous because she could see that Isis's demeanor was affecting her money. Dudes who had bills in their hands suddenly started putting them back in their pockets. Billie sat there with a shit-eating grin on her face as Isis shook her ass and made no money.

Billie was enjoying taunting Isis so much that she forgot she was waiting for Phareed. When she came back to reality, she realized that Phareed was going to want to fuck. *What the fuck am I waiting around for? I could just leave,* she thought. Billie stood up, flipped her hair at Isis, and started for the door. She got halfway across the room when someone grabbed her by the elbow.

"Yo, where you goin', ma?" Phareed said.

"I was going to the bathroom," she quickly answered.

"Let me escort you." He pulled her with him.

In the bathroom, Billie grabbed on to the edge of the sink and looked at herself in the mirror, wondering how she had gotten herself into this mess. There was no way of getting out of the club without Phareed. He was expecting to fuck once they left the club. She searched her face for an answer to her problem. How could she get out of fucking Phareed? Billie took a deep breath and exited the bathroom.

Phareed was waiting as soon as she walked out. "Let's go." He took her arm and walked her to the exit of the club. As they were exiting Billie looked behind them and saw Isis staring at them with the angriest face she had ever seen.

As soon as they were in Phareed's Hummer, Billie grabbed Phareed's dick. "You want me to suck your dick, daddy?"

"I don't get down with the little high school blowjob in the car game. I'm gonna taste all of you the proper way. I need to know what my clients are gonna be experiencing. Make sure you worth it."

"I'm on my period," she said, hoping the same lie she told Stone would work.

"I don't give a fuck. You still gonna be fuckin' for money even when you bleedin'."

Billie leaned over to start sucking his dick, hoping that once she started he would forget his "no blowjobs in the car" rule.

Phareed pushed her head back. "What I just say? You can suck my dick when we get to my crib."

Billie didn't know what else to do. She looked out the passenger window and watched the buildings pass by as she began psyching herself up to fuck Phareed. She was giving herself a pep talk and convincing herself that it would only be one time. She figured she needed to take one for the team to complete her goal.

Billie could feel the butterflies in her stomach as they pulled up in front of Phareed's crib. *Fuck it. If I'm going to do this, I might as well have fun,* she thought and exited the car.

***

"Damn! That shit was off the chain. Fuck pimpin' your ass out. I might have to keep you for myself." Phareed chuckled.

Phareed's phone started ringing. He leaned over the side of the bed and took it out of his pants pocket and looked at the caller ID.

He answered. "Hold up a minute." He looked to Billie. "Go get my weed in the closet. It's in the first drawer on the left."

Billie rolled her eyes and got out of bed.

"What up, Jumbo?" Phareed said into the phone.

Billie entered the large walk-in closet. It was filled with rows and rows of the most expensive designer clothes. The left wall of the closet had a row of six small drawers stacked on top of each other. Billie opened the top drawer and a strong smell of pot hit her nose. She picked up the Ziploc bag full of fat, green bud sitting in the front of the drawer. As she was about to close the drawer something caught her eye. In the back of the drawer was a brown leather wallet. Billie couldn't control her curiosity. She put the weed down, reached in, and took the wallet. The second she opened it up, her heart sank and her hands began to shake.

"The fuck you doin'?" Phareed grabbed the wallet out of her hand.

"Nothing." Billie put her hands behind her back so Phareed didn't see them shaking.

"I told you to get my weed, not look at my shit."

"I thought it was a cool wallet. Why don't you use it?" She gave a weak smile. Billie felt like her entire body was shaking. She wasn't sure if she was going to be able to keep control.

"Nah. This right here a souvenir. This the first nigga I ever murked." Phareed laughed, then stared at the wallet like he was thinking back to the day. He took a second, then flipped it back into the drawer like a piece of trash.

It took all of Billie's strength to not attack him right there. She wanted to slit his throat and make him suffer. She felt a tear fall from her eye. She quickly brushed past him and left the closet. Once past him she wiped the tear trickling down her cheek.

Billie frantically put her clothes on while Phareed rolled a blunt in his closet. Fully dressed, she ran down the stairs and out the door. As she was leaving she heard Phareed call for her from upstairs.

She ran as fast and as far as she could. She wanted to outrun the hurt and the pain she was feeling. When she couldn't go any farther she leaned up against the wall of an apartment building and broke down crying. All the emotions she had bottled up for the past twenty years exploded out of her in tears and wails. She was crying so hard she was convulsing. Visions of her father were running through her head. She saw him kissing her good night, she saw herself running up to him as he arrived home from work, she saw him tossing her in the air, catching her, then squeezing her with a tight hug. When the realization hit her that she had just fucked her father's killer, she threw up uncontrollably. Heave after heave of bile came spewing from the depths of her stomach. Her body was trying to purge itself of any trace of sex it had just experienced. She felt dirty, she felt stupid, she felt she betrayed her father.

After letting all of her emotions run out, Billie composed herself the best she could and started the long walk home. Her brain felt numb. As if in a trance she stared straight ahead and walked zombie-like through the streets.

When she finally made it back to her house she had no memory of how she had gotten there. She sat in her tub and let the water from the shower rain down on her. The burn from the hot water felt good to Billie. She needed to feel some pain to amend her betrayal of her father. Billie sat in the tub so long the hot water ran out and turned ice cold. Even then she didn't get out right away. More punishment for her mistake.

Billie dried off, walked into her bedroom, and collapsed on her bed. The last vision she had before she passed out was of her father, twenty years earlier, walking out the door for the last time.

# Chapter 14

Billie woke the next morning feeling like she had the worst hangover. Her head was throbbing and her body ached from all the crying she had done the night before. She popped three Advil and heated up some water for tea.

Sitting at her kitchen table, she massaged her temples, hoping that it might somehow wipe away the images of the previous night. Her teakettle whistled and ended her temple massage. She poured the boiling water into her favorite mug, but her ringing phone stopped her from sitting back down at the table.

She let out a sigh and answered the phone. "Hello."

"Billie, it's Kevin."

Billie rolled her eyes. "Kevin, I'm on a leave of absence. I'm not helping you with any of your cases. Okay?"

"That's not what I'm calling about."

Billie noticed Kevin was whispering and there was an urgency in his voice.

"What's up?" she asked.

"We are moving forward with our case against Phareed. They should be picking him up later. Thought you would want to know."

"Wait. What?" Billie was not expecting to hear that.

"I'm going to put this motherfucker behind bars."

"What time?" Billie was getting nervous.

"As soon as possible. Probably this evening."

"No." Billie covered her mouth. She didn't mean to scream the word.

"Come back to work. You can work the case with me. We can both make our names when we win."

"I gotta go."

Billie's headache was gone and her feelings of guilt disappeared too. She immediately jumped into action. She had to get to Phareed before the police. That motherfucker had to be dead, not behind bars with some bullshit sentence that would be over in no time.

In the bathroom she pulled her hair back into a ponytail, freshened up her makeup, and brushed her teeth. Her knife set went into her purse. She threw on a pair of jeans, a cream-colored blouse, some fuck-me pumps, and she was out the door. She wasn't overly concerned with her appearance. She only needed to get back into Phareed's apartment and then she could take care of business. The tricky part was going to be getting inside without anyone seeing her. It was still light out, so she couldn't operate under cover of darkness.

Billie parked her car around the block from Phareed's. She walked to the corner of his street to check things out. There were a few people walking down the street in the opposite direction. Billie didn't waste any time and started for the house. It was in the middle of the block, so she had to make it fast. She didn't want a soul seeing her anywhere near his house.

She was about a quarter of the way there when she heard police sirens. They were coming her way fast. Billie stopped and listened. The sirens were getting closer. She didn't know what to do. She had to make a decision.

Running toward the house, she planned to warn Phareed and get him safely out of there before the cops arrived. He was her prey, and no one else was going to bag him.

By the time she got in front of the house, the sirens were right around the corner. She wasn't going to make it in time. They would be there before she could even get up to the door. She was going to lose him, and other than the death of her father, this was the worst feeling she'd ever had.

The police car got to the corner and Billie started walking away, furious that she'd never get the revenge her father deserved. To her shock and delight, though, the car didn't come screeching around the corner. It kept going straight. They weren't coming for Phareed after all. Billie couldn't believe her luck. She knew it was her daddy looking down on her. With a smile on her face, she looked up to the sky and said, "Thanks, Daddy."

She composed herself and walked back to Phareed's door, ready to complete her mission. Looking around first to make sure no one was around, she knocked on the door. As she waited for Phareed for what seemed like an eternity, she kept looking in all directions, making sure it was clear.

Phareed answered the door wearing a tight white T-shirt and a pair of baggy gray Sean John sweatpants. He smiled when he saw Billie standing in front of him.

"You back for seconds?" He stepped aside for her to enter.

Billie smiled and slipped inside. She was relieved he wasn't pissed about her leaving so suddenly.

Phareed wasted no time. He grabbed her from behind and started kissing her neck. She was instantly sick to her stomach.

Billie pulled away from him. "Hold on. Let's really enjoy this. You get that weed. I'll get in bed."

"Now we talkin'." He pulled her back into him and sloppily kissed her on the lips. Even though she was repulsed, she kept her act going and kissed him back with passion. His dick jumped to attention, and he put both hands on her ass and lifted her up.

He didn't break their kiss as he carried her into the bedroom and dropped her on the bed. He reached into his sweats and pulled out his long, thick dick. It was inches from Billie's face, but she couldn't bear the thought of letting him into her mouth. She definitely wasn't going to suck his dick. Instead she grabbed it and started stroking it gently, all the while imagining herself ripping it off with her bare hands.

"I like to get fucked when I'm high, daddy. Come on. Let's blaze; then you can fuck me however you like."

"Mmmmm, a'ight, ma." He reluctantly pulled away from her grasp.

As soon as his back was turned, Billie hurriedly stripped down to her bra and underwear, took her butcher knife, and stashed it under a pillow. She leaned back in a seductive pose and waited for her target to get back from rolling a blunt. Billie pictured Phareed rolling the blunt right next to her father's wallet and it drove her mad. It was going to take every ounce of strength for her to act seductive when he returned to the bedroom.

"Hurry up," she yelled out. Billie needed to move things along. The police could be storming through the door at any minute.

"Relax, ma. You gonna get fucked." Phareed came back in the room, puffing on the blunt.

Phareed handed the blunt to Billie. "Now, where were we?" Phareed pulled his dick back out of his sweats.

"Mmmmm. You want me to suck your dick? Get over here." Billie pulled him by his waist so he was standing in front of her while she sat on the edge of the bed.

She wrapped her hand around his hard cock and took a hit from the blunt. She slid down off the bed and onto her knees and placed the blunt on top of the dresser next to the bed.

"Close your eyes," she said.

"Nah, girl, I want to watch."

"Close your eyes or you don't get any head." She gently kissed the tip of his dick.

This time he obeyed. When she saw his eyes closed she stroked his dick with one hand and reached under the pillow with the other. "You like that? You want me to suck this big dick?" she said.

"Yeah, suck my dick, baby." He moaned and leaned his head back.

Billie took hold of the butcher knife. Without hesitation she pulled it out and sliced through both of Phareed's Achilles tendons. Phareed collapsed to the ground like a rag doll, and blood immediately gushed around his feet.

"What the fuck?" he screamed.

Billie jumped up to her feet and stood over Phareed. He attempted to stand up and attack her, but the instant he put weight on his feet he collapsed again.

"You fuckin' bitch! I'ma kill you!" he screamed, even though his self-preservation instincts kicked in and he turned away from her to escape. He had lost the use of his legs, so he started to pull himself across the floor by his arms.

Billie took satisfaction in watching him struggle to get away. She slowly walked over to him and stomped on his left Achilles.

He screamed in agony. "Ahhhh! Fuck you, bitch!" The extreme pain shot straight up his leg. He flipped over on to his back and grabbed his calf muscle to try to stop the pain. Now in fight mode, Phareed swiped at Billie and tried to grab her by the leg. He badly missed, and she laughed in delight.

"You sorry motherfucker," she said through her laugh.

Billie desperately wanted to torture Phareed with a long, drawn-out process, but she was on a time limit. *No time for fun,* she thought.

"I could do this all day." She smiled.

"Fuck you," he said through gritted teeth. He flipped back on to his stomach and started to scramble away from Billie.

Billie took pleasure in watching him clumsily heave across the floor in retreat. She felt like a leopard in the Serengeti stalking its wounded prey.

Her pleasure was interrupted when she realized what Phareed was actually doing. He was scrambling for his gun. Of course, there was no chance of him making it there first. Billie slowly walked over to the dresser, picked up the 9mm, and pointed it at Phareed.

"You going for this?" she said wickedly.

Phareed stopped moving and hung his head.

"Bitch-ass punk," she said. Way off in the distance she heard a faint siren. She was sure this time those sirens were headed for Phareed. She had no more time left to play.

"Look at me," she demanded.

Phareed continued hanging his head and looking at the floor.

"Look at me!" she screamed at him.

Phareed slowly lifted his head. He had a look of evil on his face as he looked at Billie.

"Look me in the eye," she commanded. "Do you see my daddy in these eyes?"

"I don't know who your mu'fuckin' daddy is," he snarled at her.

"You should. You've got his wallet in your closet." Billie pulled the trigger—and kept pulling it another twenty times. Phareed's body convulsed every time it was hit with another bullet. Some bullets missed, but most hit their target.

Billie stared at Phareed's mangled and bloody body in disbelief. She had been chasing Phareed for so long, thinking only that he was the city's biggest drug dealer. Little did she know he was also the man who had killed her father. Now, not only had she rid the streets of a major criminal, but she had avenged her father's death. Billie felt that her father was looking down on her and had guided her to Phareed.

Police sirens getting closer snapped Billie out of her trance. She stepped over Phareed, making sure not to touch any of the blood on the floor. With tears in her eyes, she ran into the closet and got her father's wallet.

She quickly put her clothes on, threw the knife, gun, and wallet into her purse, and was out the door.

The sirens were getting louder as Billie raced down the sidewalk. Just as she arrived at the corner, the police cars passed by. Billie put her head down and kept walking as they screeched around the corner and stopped in front of Phareed's house. Billie made it to her car, threw her purse in the passenger seat, and drove off.

For a while, she kept checking her rearview to see if any cops followed her. The farther she got from Phareed's the safer she felt.

Billie drove to a park along the Delaware River and got out. She walked through the park until she came to the water's edge, where she stood and looked across to New Jersey. Reaching into her purse, she pulled out the gun and held it in front of her. A satisfied smile spread across her face. In all the years since her father's death, she'd dreamed of getting revenge, but part of her didn't believe she'd ever really get it. She figured the closest she'd ever come was making other criminals pay for the crime. In a city full of criminals, never in a million years did she think that she would find the man who murdered her father—and that she would be holding the gun that she used to exact her revenge.

She cocked her arm and threw the gun as far into the river as she could. The knife followed the gun into the river. Just as Billie was about to throw the wallet, she stopped herself. She opened the wallet and looked at her father's driver's license. There he was, smiling at her, and she knew she could never throw it away. The wallet was now Billie's souvenir.

Billie thought about the image of Phareed lying dead on the floor. It was an image she never wanted to forget. It made her happy.

# Chapter 15

The minute the police got the warrant to go after Phareed, they had split into two teams. Half of them went to the Honey Trap, and the other half went to Phareed's crib.

Walter sped down the street with his siren blaring and lights flashing. He screeched around the corner and onto Phareed's street. Out of the corner of his eye he saw a woman walking in the opposite direction. After a second it registered in his brain that the woman looked like Billie, but by the time he looked back, she had disappeared around the corner. He was almost certain it had been Billie—same profile, same walk, same style of clothing she preferred.

*What the hell is she doing in this neighborhood?* he thought.

A second later, he put her out of his mind as he screeched to a halt in front of Phareed's house, jumped out of his car, and drew his weapon. The team gathered in front of the house and stormed the front door. They spread out, going from room to room in search of Phareed.

It wasn't long before one of the team yelled out, "We've got him!"

Walter came running up the stairs to the bedroom. He stopped dead in his tracks when he saw the scene in the bedroom.

"Fuck," he said when he saw Phareed's dead body.

"This looks like it just happened. The body is still warm." The cop was feeling for a pulse. Instead of coming to arrest Phareed, they were now there to investigate a murder.

Without thinking, Walter ran downstairs, out of the house, and down the street to the corner. He looked in the direction he'd seen Billie walking, but the street was deserted.

Walter had to find out if that was really Billie he had seen, and if it was, why she was in the neighborhood? He had a strange feeling that it wasn't a coincidence.

Walter called Billie on her cell phone. No answer. He called her on her home phone. No answer. His uneasy feeling just got worse. He needed answers, and the only way to get them was to confront Billie.

Before he could go to Billie's, he needed to complete the investigation at the crime scene. While walking back to the house, he called D'Angelo. He hadn't heard from D'Angelo in more than a day. In fact, no one had heard from him, and it was beginning to worry Walter. It didn't seem to be in line with D'Angelo's character to disappear like this.

Walter left a message. "Yo, D. Where the fuck are you? Call me back."

Walter was distracted the entire time he was investigating the crime scene. He couldn't stop thinking that

D'Angelo missing and Billie being in the neighborhood were somehow connected. *Billie's in the vicinity of Phareed's house when he's murdered . . . D'Angelo is missing in action . . . What the fuck is going on?* As much as he didn't want to believe the worst, he'd been a detective long enough to know that something definitely didn't fit.

He finished with the crime scene as fast as he could. He stepped outside of the house to find that night had descended upon Philadelphia. He had been inside longer than he thought. Walter got into his car and called Billie again.

"Billie, it's Walter. Are you home?" he said after she answered.

"Yeah, why?"

"I'm coming over. Don't leave."

He hung up so quickly that Billie didn't think he even heard her say, "Okay."

During the drive to her house, Walter tried to piece together how D'Angelo and Billie could be connected— or even how Billie and Phareed might be connected. Did this have something to do with the night Billie was attacked? None of it made sense to Walter.

He parked in front of Billie's house. Usually when he arrived at her house he was excited and ready for a date. This time he felt like he was preparing to interview a suspect. He was dreading this confrontation.

Billie answered the door upbeat and relaxed. She was wearing a loose-fitting white V-neck T-shirt and a pair of tight-fitting Prada jeans.

When she saw Walter she gave him a big hug and kiss. This greeting threw Walter off. It was the opposite of what he was expecting.

"Hey. Come in." She released him and stepped aside.

"You seem to be in a good mood." He entered the house.

"I am. You want a glass of wine?"

"Sure."

Walter was feeling nervous and uncomfortable. If this had been a normal interrogation, he would have gotten right to his questioning, but this was the woman he loved. He needed answers, but he was afraid of what he might uncover. He started to have second thoughts about asking her anything.

She came back with two glasses of red wine. "How was your day?" She handed a glass to Walter.

"Good and bad." He sat on the couch.

"Oh yeah? How?" She sat next to him and pulled her feet up under her.

Walter was looking for any sign of uneasiness from Billie, but she was acting completely relaxed and normal.

"We got the go-ahead to go after Phareed today." Walter paused to see what Billie's reaction would be.

She raised her eyebrows in anticipation, but remained silent. She sipped her wine and watched him like she was watching a good movie.

"Yeah, we were all hyped to finally arrest him, but turns out we couldn't." Again Walter tried to read Billie's reaction.

"Why not? Don't tell me because of some technicality." Billie sounded aggravated.

"No. He was murdered."

"What?" Billie looked stunned. "How?"

Walter didn't want to get into specifics with Billie. It was his job to get answers from her, not the other way around.

"Billie, where were you today?" Walter's demeanor changed from casual to business. He was now in detective mode.

"Home. Why?" At the same time he slipped into his professional mode, her tone picked up an edge of nervousness.

"I called you. You didn't answer," he said.

"What time?"

"What does it matter? If you were home you would have heard the phone ring."

"It matters because I did go out for a little bit, so I was thinking it was probably then."

"I called your cell phone too."

"Well, I didn't hear it. What are you getting at?" Her body language had changed from relaxed to guarded. Her tone was definitely defensive.

"Where were you?" His tone was strict.

"I went to the grocery store."

"Which one?"

"Whole Foods."

"Where?"

"The one on North Twenty-first."

For every question Walter had, Billie had a quick answer. It was like a lightning round in a game show.

"Why did you go there?"

"'Cause I like that grocery store. You want to see my receipt? What the fuck, Walter? Just ask me whatever it is you want to ask." She was extremely angry now.

Walter couldn't tell if her anger was real or a put-on. Usually he was good at telling the difference, but his feelings for Billie were clouding his judgment.

He came right out and asked the question that he'd been wondering all along. "Were you at Phareed's house today?"

Billie paused for a second, then burst out laughing. "Are you fucking kidding me? You don't honestly think that I had anything to do with Phareed's death."

"Answer the question, Billie."

"I don't even know where he lives. How could I have been there?"

"Were you in his neighborhood?"

"If he lives near the Whole Foods on Twenty-first, then yes. Walter, what the fuck? I just told you I don't know where he lives."

"I'm just asking. I thought I might have seen you on his street. That's all."

"Well, it wasn't me. . . ." Suddenly, her anger rose to a whole new level and she jumped up from the couch. "You know what? Get the fuck out of my house!" She pointed to the door. "You come in here out of the blue and start asking me questions and trying to pin me to the murder of a drug dealer? You have lost it. Leave!"

Walter stood up, now feeling more confused than before. If this were anyone else, he would have control of his emotions and be better able to judge their truthfulness, but with Billie, his head was messed up. He couldn't set aside his feelings for her. "Billie, calm down. I'm not trying to pin anything on you. I just thought I might have seen you when I was racing toward the house. I know it sounds crazy."

"It sounds crazy because it is. Think about it. You think I could murder someone?"

Walter looked Billie in her eyes. These weren't the eyes of a killer. This was a highly educated, successful woman. He didn't want to see anything else in her eyes but goodness. He wouldn't allow himself to see anything else. No matter what his gut had been telling him earlier, he chose to believe that it wasn't Billie on the street earlier.

"Sometimes I just can't stop being a detective. You've been so distant with me, and then you go and take a leave of absence from work. I don't know, it just hasn't made sense to me. I'm not thinking straight."

"Damn right you're not thinking straight." Billie sensed she was gaining the upper hand. "You're getting so insecure about us that you're seeing things. You didn't see me anywhere today. I've told you I'm giving you as much as I can right now. If that isn't enough, then you should consider moving on."

Walter was taken aback by Billie's suggestion. "Is that what you want?"

"If that's what you want."

"No. It's not what I want." Walter was confused. How had the conversation come to this?

"Then let us be what we are going to be," Billie said gently. She took Walter's hand in hers.

"I love you." He kissed her passionately.

She pulled away from him. "Are you sure you're okay with—"

Before she could finish the sentence he kissed her again. She got her answer.

# Chapter 16

The next morning Billie was woken by her ringing cell phone. She kept her eyes closed as she clumsily felt around the nightstand for the unwelcome alarm.

Walter stirred next to her and pulled the covers under his chin.

Billie found the phone. She was lying on her side with her back facing Walter.

"Hello," she answered.

"What's up, ma?"

Billie recognized Stone's voice immediately.

"Hey." She tried to sound awake and chipper. Billie got up from the bed, went into the bathroom, and closed the door behind her. She did not want Walter hearing any part of this conversation.

"You sleeping?"

"No, no, I'm awake. How you doin'?"

"I want to see you. I still got all them clothes I bought you."

Billie had forgotten that she had left her shopping bags with Stone.

"I want to see you too, daddy. I was wondering when I was going to get those clothes from you. Where should I meet you?" She put on her sexiest voice.

"Meet me at my bar."

"What time?"

"Now."

"I'm on my way, daddy." Billie hung up the phone.

Billie wondered if Stone had heard that Phareed was dead. She figured he had, but didn't want to discuss it over the phone. She could get more information from him when she saw him.

Billie jumped in the shower and quickly washed off. When she walked back into the bedroom to get dressed, Walter was sitting up in bed. Seeing him startled Billie. She had completely forgotten he was still there.

"Good morning. Did I scare you?" he greeted her.

"I wasn't expecting you to be awake."

"Who was on the phone?"

"A girlfriend. We're going shopping." Billie avoided looking at Walter.

Walter picked up on this slight and suddenly his suspicious nature kicked back in. "Who?"

"You don't know her. Tasha. We met at my spin class."

Walter knew that Billie took an early morning spin class, but he had never heard her speak about any of the people in the class before.

"Oh. Okay. Maybe I can meet y'all for lunch," he pressed.

"Yeah, we'll see. It might just be a girls' thing though. But I'll let you know." Billie still hadn't looked at Walter. She had been busying herself with her makeup.

Walter was extremely suspicious now. He was almost certain that Billie was going to meet another man.

"All right. I gotta go home." Walter got out of bed and started dressing.

Billie continued with her makeup and hair as Walter finished dressing.

"Call me," Walter said as he left the bedroom.

Billie was surprised that Walter didn't even kiss her good-bye. She thought about it for a second then quickly dropped it. She didn't have time to worry about any of that. She had to get her game face on and meet with Stone to find out what he knew about Phareed's death.

Billie thought about her chance meeting with Stone as she drove to the bar. She was at an extremely low point when she walked into the bar that day. She had just been attacked, was bloodied and bruised and un-certain about her next moves. Then fate took over and Stone showed up. What were the odds that she would need a drink and go to the bar owned by Stone? She was sure the odds were high, but again she thought of her daddy and was certain that he was leading her from above.

Billie pulled up in front of the bar. No lights were on and the metal security gates were still down in front of the windows. She was a little hesitant to enter the bar, but ignored any fear she had.

Stone was sitting at the empty bar when she walked in. He was the only one there. He got up from his stool and walked toward Billie, meeting her halfway. He grabbed her waist and kissed her right away. Their tongues explored each other's mouths in a passionate embrace.

Billie was not ready but quickly settled in and went along with it. From this greeting she knew that she had Stone where she wanted him. She was going to be able to manipulate this entire encounter.

They broke their embrace. "Mmmm that was a nice hello," said Billie.

Stone put his hands on her shoulders and leaned forward to whisper in her ear. "Phareed is dead." He paused and remained leaning into her. She could feel his breath in her ear. "And you killed him."

Before Billie had time to react, Stone shoved her hard. She slammed into the tables behind her, and chairs scattered as she ended up splayed out on the floor.

"You think you can get away with this? You cheating, murdering bitch!" He raced forward and kicked her in the stomach like a punter kicking a field goal in football.

She gasped audibly as the wind was knocked out of her. She lay in the fetal position on the floor, wheezing and coughing and clutching her stomach, struggling to regain control of her breath.

"What . . . are . . . you . . . talking . . . about?" she said.

"You know exactly what I'm talkin' 'bout, bitch." He kicked her again. This time her arm was in the way to protect her stomach and absorb the blow.

Stone grabbed her by the back of her shirt and picked her off the floor like a doll.

"I didn't kill anyone." She was crying, trying to deal with the pain in her stomach. She couldn't figure out how Stone could know she killed Phareed. Had she left a clue? *Deny 'til you die,* she told herself.

"Fuck you, you lying bitch!"

Billie heard Isis's voice behind her and then felt Isis's fist to the back of her head. "I saw your grimy ass leave the club with Phareed. Next thing you know he dead!" Another punishing blow connected to the back of Billie's head.

Billie saw stars and heard a ringing in her ears. She was on the verge of passing out. She fought back but was unsuccessful. Next thing she knew, her world went black.


She came to, but was completely disoriented. It took her a second to get her bearings. She had no idea what had just happened or how long she had been out. When she began to regain her wits, she realized she was still in Stone's grasp, getting hit in her face.

"Wake up, bitch." Stone was slapping her over and over. "Isis, get me water to throw in this bitch's face."

As Isis started for the bar, the front door flew open.

"Philadelphia PD. Hands up." Walter came bursting through the front door and charged directly at Stone.

Isis bolted for the back door.

Stone threw Billie to the ground and tried to run, but Walter had too much of a head start and easily caught up with him. Walter tackled Stone, and the two started fighting.

Billie was still attempting to recover from passing out. Her head was foggy and her body felt weak.

Watching the two men fight had a dreamlike quality for Billie.

Walter and Stone were in a vicious battle. Tables were getting knocked around, chairs were flying, and heads were being pummeled. The men were trading punches back and forth, each one wrestling to gain control over the other. It was like two bears fighting for dominance.

Walter finally gained the upper hand and pinned Stone on his stomach. He was able to twist one of Stone's arms behind his back and attach a handcuff around his wrist. He grabbed hold of the other wrist and clamped it in the cuff.

"Get the fuck off me!" Stone yelled.

Walter picked Stone up off the ground. Billie's head was clearer as she stood and stabilized herself on her feet. Walter pushed Stone toward the door. As they passed Billie, Stone said, "Fuck you, Sheila. You think you can get away with murdering Phareed? You a dead bitch!"

Walter hit Stone in the back of his head and pushed him out the door, giving Billie a curious look as he passed her. Still trying to process everything that had just happened, Billie walked behind the bar and poured herself some vodka. Even though it was still early in the day, she needed something to steady her nerves.

She sat at the bar with her head in her hands until the front door opened up. Billie turned her head to see Walter coming back into the bar. He had locked Stone in the car.

"Billie, what the fuck was he talking about? What is going on?"

"I don't know."

"Don't fuck with me!" Walter screamed and slammed his hand on the bar, startling Billie. Walter saw her reaction and calmed himself. "Look, I love you Billie. I have been patient and I have tried to be understanding these past few weeks when something's obviously been going on with you. Now I need you to be honest with me. What is he talking about you killing Phareed?"

Billie heard what he said, and, looking into his eyes, she wanted to be honest with him. But of course she knew she could never be, not about this. So she put her best game face on, and said, "I honestly don't know. You heard him. He called me Sheila. He thinks I'm someone else. But think about it. That makes sense. You thought you saw me the other day near Phareed's house. It must be the same woman who this guy is confusing me with."

Walter thought about this for a second. It could make sense, but he wasn't convinced. After all, what the hell was she doing in this bar with that thug?

"Why are you here? At this bar so early? I thought you were meeting your friend to go shopping." He actually sounded disappointed, like a father who just realized his daughter has been lying to him.

"I . . . I was . . . just . . . Look, I can't lie to you, Walter. I was coming in here for a drink. I've been under a lot of stress."

Walter looked at the empty glass sitting on the bar in front of her. Again, it could make sense, but there were too many pieces that didn't fit.

"Are you fucking this guy?"

"No!"

"Billie, be straight with me."

Billie sensed that Walter wasn't buying her story. She didn't think she could keep making up excuses without messing up. Then it hit her—turn it on him.

"Wait, what are you doing here? You didn't just happen in on this bar. Were you fucking following me?" she asked indignantly.

She had nailed him. She could see it on his face. Walter's facial expression went from stern to worried.

"No, I, um . . ." He was searching for words.

"I can't believe it. How long have you been following me?"

"Just today. I swear. I got suspicious this morning and I decided to follow you."

"I can't deal with this, Walter. I'm done. You're suffocating me." She was just so relieved that he had stopped asking questions. She didn't really want to end things with him, but in the moment, she just wanted to get the fuck out of this situation.

Walter wasn't going to be sent away that easily. "Don't turn this on me," he said.

Feeling like she was running out of options, Billie got up from the bar and walked out the front door. Walter followed her.

"Billie," he called to her.

She ignored him and kept walking, got into her car, and pulled away.

Walter watched her drive off, turn the corner, and disappear. He hadn't gotten the full story from her and he knew it. What he didn't know was whether he really wanted to hear the real story.

"Looks like you got played, nigga," Stone said as Walter got in the car.

"Shut the fuck up." Walter pulled away from the curb and headed to the station house to process Stone.

# Chapter 17

Walter sat at his desk, wringing his hands. He hadn't slept all night thinking about his past few confrontations with Billie. Something wasn't adding up and it was making him uneasy. He had a decision to make. Would he investigate further or just be content knowing that some things might be better left untouched? His loyalty to his job and his affection for Billie were at odds with each other.

Walter placed his hand on his computer keyboard and opened the files of all the recent murders of Phareed's men.

Walter's captain walked up to his desk. "Any word from D'Angelo?"

"No, sir," Walter replied.

"Finding him is your top priority. Drop everything else."

"Yes, sir."

With that, Walter had his answer. He had a bad feeling about D'Angelo. He knew that a cop who'd been missing for more than forty-eight hours was not a good sign, and this investigation could be open for a good long while. In the meantime, other cases would come across his desk. He wouldn't be able to "drop everything else" indefinitely. Hell, in this city he probably wouldn't be able to drop anything else by the time lunch rolled around.

Phareed was dead. Stone was behind bars, and Billie . . . Well, he'd have to see if he could mend things with Billie. He had high hopes for them. He thought they could make it work. The woman drove him crazy sometimes, sure, but that wasn't always a bad thing, and he couldn't help how deeply in love he'd fallen with her. He'd always put his job first, but a tiny voice in the back of his head asked him: just this one time, given all the circumstances, wouldn't it be better to put his heart first?

Walter opened D'Angelo's investigation file while, in his mind, he closed Billie's.


Across town, Billie walked into District Attorney Stanley Lewis's office. "I'm ready to come back to work," she said.

"When?"

"Immediately."

Stanley Lewis rose from his desk put his hand out and said, "Good to have you back. Let Kevin catch you up to speed."

Billie shook his hand, then left his office without another word. She went back to her office and closed the door behind her. It felt like it had been an eternity since she had been there.

She picked up the phone and dialed.

"Hello?" the elderly woman answered.

"Mama, it's Billie. Daddy's killer is dead. Justice has finally been served." A lone tear trickled down Billie's cheek.

Excerpt from
The Family Business 2
by Carl Weber with Treasure Hernandez

# Prologue

It was late when attorney Harris Grant, accompanied by his wife London, entered the corporate headquarters of Duncan Motors. The two maneuvered through the dimly lit exotic car showroom, then along the dark corridors of offices until they reached the board room. Harris had tried to convince London, who was due to give birth to their second child any day now after a difficult pregnancy, to stay home and relax. London refused, arguing that she had a responsibility as a stockholder and a member of the Duncan Motors board of directors to attend the emergency meeting of the board. Concerned that arguing would stress his pregnant wife more than she already was, Harris reluctantly agreed. He did, however, feel that his wife's insistence to attend the meeting had more to do with her being nosey and wanting to be in the loop than her sense of responsibility and duty to the company.

Already in attendance were London's siblings—Rio, the company's director of marketing and promotion; Junior, the company's head of security; and Paris, the company's trouble shooter, who was also about ready to pop with child. By the time Harris had helped his wife to her seat and taken his, London's father, Lavernius Duncan Sr., or L.C. as he liked to be called, entered the board room. An imposing figure in his late sixties, L.C. was the founder of Duncan Motors and chairman of the board. Known for his explosive temper, L.C. was not a man you wanted to anger for any reason, and he didn't look happy as he scanned the room. His eyes stopped briefly when they reached his youngest daughter, Paris, who quickly removed her shoes from the boardroom table. When L.C.'s gaze rested on an empty chair at the table, Junior, the oldest child, shared a knowing glance with Harris. Conspicuous in his absence was the man who had summoned them all to this meeting, the company's new CEO, Orlando Duncan.

"Where's Orlando?" the elder Duncan barked. He was holding out a chair for his wife, Chippy, who had followed him into the room.

The room fell silent until Rio, the youngest son and twin to Paris, said, "He went to get something out of his lab, Pop. He said to tell you he'd be here in a minute."

Rio's explanation did not help L.C.'s mood. "What's he doing in his lab?" he snapped. "Is that where he's been the past few weeks? He's supposed to be running this company, not dissecting frogs."

Rio shrugged, slumping back in his chair. "You gotta talk to him about that, Pop. I'm just relaying the message."

L.C. started grumbling something under his breath. It was obvious that he was not happy about Orlando calling an emergency meeting in the middle of the night and then not being there when he and the other board of directors arrived.

Chippy spoke up for her son. "You're the one who wanted them all to have specialties outside their jobs with the company," she said. "You know him, he's probably got some experiment running that needs to be checked on every couple of hours. He'll be here soon."

Like most parents, L.C. had a vision for his children and watched them all very closely as they grew up. He helped and pushed them to hone their interests and abilities no matter what they were. He wanted each of them to have an expertise outside the car business or specialties as he called them, that they could fall back on. In Orlando's case his specialty was chemistry, which he held a master's degree in along with a pharmaceutical license.

"Finally," Paris huffed, when Orlando walked into the room five minutes later. He was still wearing a lab coat as he carried a briefcase in one hand and small brown paper bag in the other.

"I know, I know, sorry I'm late," Orlando apologized then gestured for Junior to close the doors to the room as he took his seat. "I'm sure you're all wondering why I called this meeting and more importantly why I didn't just have it at home or during our next scheduled meeting next month. I thought about that but I wanted to give you all the good news right away."

L.C. sat back in his chair rocking it. "Ok, then son what's this good news you've got?"

A huge grin took over Orlando's face before he spoke, "I've done it, Pop. I've fucking done it! After all these years I've finally done it!"

He stopped himself looking each of his family members in the eyes before moving to the next. He now had this crazy smile that with his lab coat he was wearing, made him look like a mad scientist that had lost his mind. L.C.'s first thought was that his son may have had had some kind of breakdown. He wasn't the only one who had come to that conclusion either because his outspoken daughter Paris said what he was thinking.

"Yo, O, you been sniffing that shit you be making over at the lab or something? 'Cause bro, your ass is talkin' real crazy. Keep it up and I'm gonna check your ass into Creedmoor for a psychic evaluation." She gave him the universal sign for crazy, twirling her index finger at the side of her head. More than one person at the table laughed including their mother.

"I'm not crazy Paris. Am I Rio?" he tilted his head in his younger brother's direction and all eyes turned to Rio.

"No, O you're not crazy. You're not crazy at all." Rio and Paris were usually the least mature of the Duncan clan but this time Rio sat up straight in his chair, articulating his message clear and professionally. "What you are about to do is make us all filthy fucking rich."

"We already are rich," Paris spat skeptically.

"No little sister, we are nigger rich," Orlando said firmly turning his attention from Paris back to L.C. "I'm about to make us Donald trump . . . Bill Gates rich . . . Warren Buffet rich. I'm talking about billionaire rich."

There was an eerie silence in the room until L.C. said, "Son, what the hell are you talking about?"

"You got that thing on?" Orlando glanced over at his older brother Junior who nodded.

As the head of the family's security Junior had the board room and his father's office outfitted with electronic jamming devices. Even if prying ears wanted to, they couldn't listen to the Duncan's board room conversations. The device was so powerful you couldn't even use a cell phone in those rooms when they were turned on.

The fact that Orlando was making sure his conversation wouldn't be overheard let everyone in the room know that he was about to talk about the Duncan family's dirty little secret. A secret they'd kept hidden from both law enforcement and the general public. You see the Duncan's weren't just successful car dealers, they were also one of the nation's largest illegal distributors of narcotics on the east coast.

Orlando stood in front of his family purposely hesitating for dramatic affects before he spoke. For him, today was like Christmas Day and he was Santa Claus about to give them the biggest Christmas present of all. He glanced over at his mother who smiled proudly at him. She'd always been his biggest supporter, reinforcing in him that he could do anything if he put his mind to it. His father on the other hand was not as easily impressed but for the first time in his life he wasn't worried about that, because once he finished his presentation he was sure L.C. Duncan would be kissing his ass.

"For the last thirty years we've been the ultimate middle man distributing other people's product around the eastern United States through our dealerships and transport businesses. Now don't get me wrong we've made a lot of money being a distributor. It's a good business and we're good at it but wouldn't it be nice if we didn't have to pay for the product we distribute? Wouldn't it be nice if we ran not only the distribution side of the business but the manufacturing and production side as well, Pop?"

The two of them stared at eachother until a smile creped across L.C.'s face and he nodded his head at his son. "You got my attention son. What exactly do you have in mind?"

"This!" Orlando picked up the paper bag he'd carried into the room emptying its contents onto the board room table. At least a hundred red M&M's came sprawling across the table. "Ladies and gentlemen of the Duncan family . . . I give you H.E.A.T."

L.C. stared at the M&M's and frowned. "What the hell is this some kind of joke?"

"I ain't complaining, I been craving M&M's all week." Paris reached out to pick up a handful. She'd barely closed her hand around the candies before Rio grabbed her wrist.

"Don't eat that!" he yelled squeezing tight.

Paris yanked back her arm. "Why? What the fuck is wrong with them?"

"Those aren't M&M's," Rio scolded.

"Then what the fuck are they?" Paris snapped.

"Orlando, what the hell's going on?" L.C. demanded. He picked up a handful of the candy look-a-likes then dropped them on the table. "What is this crap?"

"I call it H.E.A.T., Pop." He held one in his hand. "It's the new crack. No, actually its better than crack. It's extremely potent synthetic pheromones and endorphins laced with morphine and its gonna make us wealthy beyond your wildest dreams."

Harris gave his brother-in-law a cynical look. "Excuse me if I sound doubtful, but we've heard that before?"

"Harris is right. What makes these things so special?" L.C. asked.

"It's a high no user has ever seen. The drug seems to take them to the same place of exhilaration that crack or meth does for about an hour without physical addiction nor withdrawal. Some test subjects have experienced mental addiction on the level of marijuana. To make it simple they can't get enough of this stuff."

"He ain't lying, Pop," Rio sat up in his chair. "He gave me five hundred of these things and I gave half of them to the club dealers to give away last Friday. The next day dealers were buying them wholesale five dollars a pill with a retail price of ten bucks and they were begging me for more by the end of the night. Now the whole sale price is $10 a pill and demand is so high if I want I can raise the price at any time. We can barely keep up with demand. I must have sold five thousand already and that's being conservative. I'm telling you these little red M&M's are a gold mind."

Harris leaned forward in his chair. You could see the excitement in his eyes. There was no doubt he could see the potential in the new drug. "What's the manufacturing cost?"

"Right now about a buck a pill but once we gear up production I can get it to about thirty-five cents," Orlando relied.

Harris reached down into his briefcase pulling out a calculator. He punched in some numbers then stared at the results. He looked like he might have done something wrong so he punched the numbers in again. "Holy shit!" he said turning the calculator in the direction of L.C. who was seated next to him.

L.C. glanced at the numbers then did a double take, removing the calculator from Harris's hand. "Is that yearly?"

Harris shook his head. "Nope, that's monthly, using just our domestic network numbers. If we go outside the network you can triple possibly even quadruple that number. And that's not including overseas."

L.C. sat back in his chair playing with his goatee as he contemplated the information that had been presented to him. It wasn't the type of thing that happened often, but he actually looked impressed.

"Have you tested for side effects?" London chirped in. Her nursing background and family specialty coming out. "Synthetic drugs usually have side effects."

"Yes, extensively London, there are no side effects that we can see other than the user sleeping for long periods after consecutive use. Like I said before, it's not physically addictive, but it can be mentally addictive." He opened his briefcase and handed her a folder. London skimmed through it as Orlando continued.

"Pop it's the ultimate recreational drug with no side effects." Orlando said. "The yuppies can use it all week-end long and with a good night's sleep go to work on Monday feeling fine."

L.C. turned to Harris. "Ok, Mr. Grant you're our legal counsel, what do you think?"

"You saw the numbers, L.C. and numbers don't lie. If Orlando and Rio are anywhere close to being correct about demand and production cost, this is a no-brainer. We can't afford not to be involved, there's too much money at stake." Harris replied confidently.

"How much money we talking about Harris?" Junior asked.

"We could make our first billion within a year and that's just in the US market." Harris smiled. "Smart thing to do is set up a factory outside the US. Buy a small South American pharmaceutical company under a shell corp to do all the manufacturing. We can do it here for a while but once this thing goes national we're gonna wanna put some distance and corporations between it and us. We might wanna bring in some of your Cuban and Colombian friends as fronts to give us some cover, L.C. We're also going to need quite a few legitimate companies to launder the amount of new cash we're gonna pull in."

Junior whistled then said, "A billion dollars. Damn that's a lot of bread.

"No, that's a lot of shopping," Paris injected dancing in her chair. She raised her hand and Rio high-fived her.

"That's enough out of you two." L.C. spat then turned his attention to his older daughter. "London, anything in that report that we should be worried about?"

"Nothing that I can see Daddy. He's done a pretty thorough job and all the proper tests. From the looks of it, Orlando's right; he's created the perfect drug."

L.C. nodded his head. "You've done good here, Orlando. Real good. I'm proud of you, son."

Orlando beamed. "Thanks Pop."

L.C. looked around the room smiling for the first time since he'd entered the room. "Well, I say we go forward with this new H.E.A.T. venture. Harris you start putting together the corporations and the legal protection we'll need. I'm thinking we should buy a couple of big rig dealerships in the Midwest and down south to launder some of this money? Oh, and set up a meeting with some of the law enforcement folks we have on payroll. Probably time some of them got new cars."

"I'm on it L.C.," Harris replied.

"Orlando, you gear up manufacturing on a small scale for now, until Harris can buy us a pharmaceutical company south of the border. Junior, put together a security plan. If this takes off there are going to be more people than normal coming after us. When they do, I want them to know that the Duncan's are not to be played with. Also, I want Orlando's lab to have 24 hour armed guards."

"What about me, Pop?" Rio sounded annoyed. Once again he felt like his father was leaving him out because of his sexuality.

The two Duncan men locked eyes until L.C. said, "I didn't forget you Rio. I want you to go on a little road trip to our club down in South Beach. See if you get the same response down there from H.E.A.T. that you got up here. Personally, I'd like to start distribution outside of the northeast, away from our normal base of operation."

L.C. glanced around the room. "Any objections before I close the meeting?"

"Yes, I have an objection. I have a big objection." The person who spoke was the most unlikely voice in the room.

# LC

## 1

The room had fell silent as my wife Chippy rose from the chair next to mine. You didn't hear much from her at these board meetings lately, except to occasionally chastise the twins Rio or Paris for speaking out of turn. She'd been under the weather for the better part of a year now. Her passion lately seemed to be more with the wellbeing of our children and grandchildren and less and less with the day to day running of our family business. However, her objection to Orlando's new drug rang loud and clear. She might as well have run up behind me and pulled my pants down to my ankles because I didn't see it coming at all. I can count on one hand the number of times Chippy had spoken out against me in front of our children without warning when it came to business. We always seemed to be on the same page but from her tone we were far from being on the same page today.

"Are you serious?" Orlando asked in disbelief. If you think I was caught off guard you should have seen the look on his face. He looked like someone had hit him in the back of the head with a sledgehammer and just realized that the someone was his very own mother.

"Yes, Orlando very serious. I know this is important to you and I'm sorry, but I just can't get behind this," Chippy replied. Both her demeanor and body language challenged our sons authority.

"But, Ma, why?" Orlando whined irately.

"Because it's not safe. We've operated below the police and the Feds radar for almost thirty years. Something like this is going to bring them to our front door. You mark my words . . ."

"Chippy," I interrupted, "let me worry about the cops. I can take care of it . . ."

"I'm talking to my son," she snapped. She raised her hand dismissing me and the look on her face made me take a step back. It was something I did not like and would address on the ride home "Nothing you can say is going to change my mind on this, L.C. Your greedy and selfishness almost got Rio killed last year. I'm not about to let you put my other children in that position too. I don't give a damn how much money is involved." Yes, we would be addressing all of this later, of that I had no doubt. I just hoped I was the one in control of the conversation.

"But, Ma, this isn't just about money. It's an opportunity of a lifetime," Orlando tried not to sound like he was pleading with his mother but there was no doubt about the desperation in his voice. "H.E.A.T. will set up the Duncan family for the next five generations. Besides, it's no different than what we already do, except we won't have to kiss anybody's ass for product anymore. They'll be kissing ours."

"Are you that naïve? 'Cause from where I'm sitting your opportunity opens us up to a whole lot more exposure. Not only from the authorities but from everyone else too. Do you really think the Italians or the Jews or the other black families for that matter are going to kiss your black ass? 'Cause I can assure you they won't. What they will do is fight to take what you made. I, for one, don't think we're ready for that."

I wasn't one to feel sorry for anyone but I felt sorry for my son. His mother had been his biggest supporter when we made the decision to make him the new head of the family business. Now it looked like she was turning on him.

"You're not sure we're ready for that or I'm ready for that, Ma? Which one is it?" Orlando confronted his mother. "If Vegas was sitting in this chair would you be objecting to this?"

"If Vegas were here we wouldn't be having this conversation. The plan always was for him to take over that side of our operation and for you to run the legitimate side. I never wanted this for you." She might have well had ripped out the boys heart, right in front of us. Because we all knew what she was saying without her saying. I just didn't know she felt so strongly about it until today. I'm pretty sure the rest of the family didn't either.

"Charlotte," I said using her government name to loosen the tension. "There's nothing to worry about. Orlando's perfectly capable of handling things. Besides, I'll be here to help him. So will Harris and Junior."

She glanced at my son-in-law and my oldest son then shook her head back and forth. "Is that supposed to comfort me? Do you have any idea what you're having my son locked away for that shit you did has done to my family?" I was trying to collect my thoughts so I could talk some reason into her but she had just hit below the belt.

"Ohhhhhhhhhhhhh," London squealed. All attention turned to my oldest daughter who was holding her round belly looking up at her husband. "Harris, I think you better go get the car because it's time."

I glanced over at Chippy who within a matter of seconds was at London's side. Her face was now riddled with motherly concern. While the uncompromising demeanor she had towards Orlando and myself was completely gone. Orlando on the other hand was still standing at the head of the table with the same look of disbelief that he'd worn when his mother first made her objection.

# Sasha

## 2

I'd been circling the block for the better part of ten minutes before a parking space opened up in front of Rocky's BBQ. I slid on my shades and checked my pink shoulder length wig in the rearview mirror before refreshing my pink lipstick. I looked pretty damn fierce if I do say so myself, so I step out the car surveying the street. It was late, almost ten minutes to ten, so most the people in neighborhood were either in their homes or on their way home. I headed towards the neon lit restaurant.

The sign above the door read, *Rocky's Home of Chitown's Best Ribs*. They didn't have to spell it out for me. I hadn't had anything to eat since breakfast, so it didn't matter to me if they were the worst ribs in Chicago I planned on having some with cornbread and collard greens.

Surprisingly, for a place that boosted having the best ribs in town, the place was damn nearly empty when I walked in. It was a good thing because I hated crowds. Aside from the Robocop looking dude behind the counter and the Puerto Rican cook, there were three loud mouth guys in the back half of the place along with an old man in the corner eating some BBQ chicken like it was going out of style. There was no doubt I was gonna have some of that.

I leaned on the counter giving the simple menu the once over.

"What you having?" The guy behind the counter asked. He was at least 6'4 two hundred and seventy-five pounds with a weight-lifters body. He gave me a look like he'd been doing this shit way too long and didn't have no patience for any BS. He really did look like Robocop.

"Let me have some of that chicken he's eating, and a rack of ribs with a side of collard greens and cornbread to go." I offer a half smile, which immediately softened his demeanor like I had passed some test or something. His eyes never left my body thanks to my snug hot pink low cut running top, black tights, and hot pink sneakers, which showed off my flawless C-cups, phat round booty and athletic legs, perfectly. If I wanted him, he could be mine in a matter of minutes.

"You want mac and cheese or a drink with that?" he asked jotting down my order.

"No. I'm good. I got water in the car." My response is more flirtatious than before. "Are your ribs as good as Carson's? I been to Carson's and their ribs are finger licking good."

"Fuck Carson's! Our ribs are the best in Chicago." He laughed handing the cook my order.

"Where's your restroom?" I smiled up at him, which isn't that much of a stretch since I'm 5'10" in my bare feet. He pointed to a door in the back. I gave him another flirtatious smile then strutted past the old man who was eating his chicken. When I got close to the table with three men, all conversation ceased as I walked by, that is until they saw my butt.

"Look at the ass on her," I heard one of them say under his breath."

"You a ribs kinda girl?" one of them said, in more of a Brooklyn accent than Chicagoan. He was not speaking under his breath. I stopped and turned making sure I gave him the best view. He was the cutest of the three and probably the best dressed although they are all wearing suits. "You don't look like a ribs kinda girl."

His buddies who were now standing behind me never took their gaze off my hips; I could practically feel their eyes touching my ass. Not that it was a problem because a girls gotta be honest with herself: you don't wear an outfit like this if you don't expect to attract attention.

"Oh yeah, what kind of girl do I look like," I flirted shamelessly.

He stared me in the eyes, confidently. "You look like the kind of woman who would enjoy champagne and caviar, dinner on the French Rivera, oh and most importantly, making love on yacht in the middle of the Caribbean."

My smile broadened. He really was talking my language.

I leaned over placing both hands on the table he was sitting at to show him more cleavage. I wasn't into white boys but this one actually showed promise. "And you can make that happen?"

"Sweetheart, I can make that happen and more."
He extended his hand with a smile. "My names Mike
Nugent."

"My names Sasha," I replied taking his hand with a
giddy smile.

"Forget the ribs, Sasha," he said smoothly, "let me
take you to a real restaurant, someplace with atmosphere and a five star menu."

"You know what, Mike, I like the way you talk," I
smiled pointing at the restroom door. "Now hold that
thought, I'll be right back, okay."

I gave him a wink and he sat back in his chair like he
owned the joint. "I'll be waiting," he said confidently.

I swing my hips like a supermodel on the runway as I
make my way to the restroom. I can hear them talking
as I pull my pants down to relieve myself.

"Holy shit, Mikie, she's fuckin' beautiful. She looks
like that rapper chick, Nikki Manaj. Jezzze, I'd pay to
fuck a broad like her."

"Well, Pauli to bad you're not me cause I'm gonna
fuck the shit outta her for free," Mikie replied.

I smile at the thought. In his mind he'd already
had me in bed, probably already saw me on my knees
sucking his dick in preparation for me taking it from
behind. It wasn't the worst thing anyone had ever
thought when it came to me but I had other ideas for
Mr. Mikie Nugent because nothing was ever free.

After washing my hands I placed my bag on the sink
securing what I need at the top before throwing it back
over my shoulder. I made one last quick check in the
bathroom mirror before opening the door, a girl had to
look good when she made her grand entrance.

Mike smiled watching my hips as I walked out the bathroom door. His boys were just standing there gawking at my breast then my ass as I pass.

"So what's it gonna be doll, Italian, Greek, seafood, you name it?" he asked with even more confidence.

"Sorry to say this, but I'm thinking about just taking the ribs I ordered home," I said sincerely reaching in my purse, "I would ask for a rain check, but you're going to be dead in the next five seconds." He gave me the most puzzled look as I raised a silenced pistol from my bag towards his head. They were all so damn busy looking at my tits and ass they didn't pay any attention to my hands.

"Oh shit, Pauli, it's a hit!" Mikie yelled.

I smiled pulling the trigger, a second later a bullet was lodged between Mikie's eyes and he fell back in his chair. I'm sure he was dead before he hit the ground. Instinctively I spun taking both his boys out with two shots a piece as they reached in there suit jackets for weapons.

It was over except for the old man, the cook and Robocop at the counter. The old man immediately raised his hands the second I looked in his direction. I gestured for him to get on the floor and he did what he was told. He was no threat so I began to walk toward the front door and the exit. The cook wasn't stupid either he dropped to the floor the second he saw me coming guns a-blazing, which made him no threat. But I could tell from his body language, that Robocop was going to be a problem, he was going to be a big fucking problem. It was never more evident than when he jumped over the counter holding a sawed off shot gun.

"You bitch, those guys owed me ten grand from the Bears game. Now whose gonna pay me my money?" he asked irately.

Normally I would have just put two in his grill and walked the fuck out but I'd done what I was supposed to do. Things had worked out way better than I could have expected, because originally I was just expecting Mike to be at Rocky's, I never expected his partners Peter Mann and Leo Garza to be around too. My contract was complete, there was no need for anyone else to die, that is unless Robocop wanted to push the issue.

"Trust me mister, they would have never paid you. Why do you think I'm here? They owe my employer over 500 grand."

"I don't give a damn how much they owed other people. They were going to fucking pay me," he swore.

"Oh yeah, when? How come they haven't paid you yet? The game was Monday night; it's Thursday now. Mister they weren't going to pay. I doubt they have a thousand bucks between them. They're a bunch of coked out losers. Or at least they use to be."

"Well, bitch then you're going to pay me." He took a step towards me.

"Mister, I don't like being called a bitch. Matter a fact, I've killed people for less. Now drop the fucking shot gun so I can get by."

"I want my money!" he took a step closer. Well, at least this time he dropped the bitch out of it.

"Look, I don't have a lot of time. Either you drop the gun or I make you drop it. "

"Who the fuck you think you are Annie Oakley?" he sounded angry, but he looked more confused and actually took another step closer.

"Hell no. Annie Oakley ain't even in my fucking league." I pulled the trigger to my gun shooting his hand. He dropped the shot gun screaming in pain.

"You shot me! You fucking bitch. You fucking shot me!"

"What did you just call me? Didn't I tell you not call me a bitch?" A swift kick to his groin dropped him to the floor. "You ungrateful bastard you could be dead right now. I coulda killed you instead of shooting your hand. Now stay down or be dead!" He looked up at me gripping his injured hand then let his body merge into the floor.

I was just about to walk out when I spotted a bag on the counter. "Hey, is that my order?" When I didn't get an answer I repeated myself placing a little more bass in my voice. "Are those my ribs?"

"Yeah," the cook said from the floor behind the counter. "Those are your ribs."

"Great, how much do I owe you for them?"

"They're on the house," the cook replied.

I glanced over at Robocop, "Is that cool with you?"

"Yeah, just get the fuck outta here."

"Wow, thanks," I snatch up my order and head out onto the sidewalk, stashing my gun back in my bag as I made a quick rush for my car.

Five minutes later I was in a parking garage switching vehicles and removing the tacky sunglasses, and the wig. I'd just finished changing in the backseat when my cell phone rang.

"Yes," I said into the phone.

"I have been told the job has been completed." a deep eastern Indian accented voice asked.

"It has," I replied.

"Then I will arrange for the second half of your payment to be delivered in the normal fashion, along with the first half of your next assignment."

"Next assignment? I was hoping to get a little R&R, maybe a week or two off for vacation. I've been at this for six straight months."

"I am sorry, Ms. Sasha, but that is not possible. Your next assignment is very important to our employer. It must be completed as soon as possible."

"I hear you. Look, just let them know that a sister needs a little time off for herself."

"I will convey your message and make arrangements for your flight in the morning. Good night."

"Yeah, you too." I hung up the phone and finished getting dressed. Well, at least with my flight leaving in the morning there was the possibility of hooking up tonight and getting laid.

# Paris

## 3

"This shit just ain't fair," I whined. My twin brother Rio and I had just sat down to eat at the Au Bon Pain sandwich shop at Long Island Jewish Medical Center where London was having her baby. My own baby had been kicking the shit out of me because she was hungry. So I damn near dragged Rio with me to get something to eat after we'd been sitting in the hospital waiting room almost two hours with the rest of the family.

"What ain't fair?" Rio asked scooping two spoons full of soup out of a bread bowl.

"That London's having her baby before I'm having mine. We had the same damn due date." I sighed ripping open a second packet of mustered and spread it all over a piece of French bread. "Her ass is always trying to outdo me in front of Daddy. I know she did that shit on purpose. She just wanted her baby to be older than mine."

Rio picked up his sandwich, took a bite and laughed. "Gurrrrrlll, are you for real? Do you really think she went into labor in the middle of a board of directors meeting, while Ma was on the war path I might add, just to piss you off?"

He gave me a skeptical look, but I replied quickly.

"I wouldn't put it past her. She's a nurse ain't she? She probably figured out some way to induce labor before she even got to the meeting."

"Why, because that's what you would do?" he was half-heartedly joking, but my lack of response and the smirk on my face gave him the answer he was looking for. "No! Girl, you need to stop. You were not going to induce labor just to make sure you had your baby before London?"

"The hell I wasn't. I was supposed to see the doctor tomorrow but that sneaky bitch London beat me to it. I know she did." Just thinking about her trying to outdo me in front of my father pissed me off.

"Not everyone is as calculating as you, Paris." Rio took another bite of his sandwich.

I stopped and stared at him. "What's that supposed to mean? I know you're not taking her side because you're supposed to be my twin." Not only was Rio my twin he was like my best girlfriend. I could talk to him about anything and I mean anything. I guess it didn't hurt that he was gay.

"Girl, I ain't taking nobody's side in this one. You both my sisters and I love you, you know that."

"But you love me more, right?" I tilted my head and smiled waiting for my brothers' answer. I loved putting him on the spot. "Right?"

He nodded, "Yeah, you my twin, my other half, I got to love you more, but that don't mean I don't love London too."

I smirked my approval, taking a bite out of my mustered and bread sandwich, savoring the taste. I'd been craving mustard and bread all day. "Oh my God. This is so good. You have got to try it!"

I lifted my sandwich up towards his face and he backed away, waving his hand. "No thanks. I don't know how you can eat bread and mustered with no meat. That's nasty if you ask me." He made a face.

"I'm pregnant silly. I can eat just about anything, if I'm in the mood. And this is so good." I took another bite then laughed lifting the sandwich towards his face again just to watch him squirm. I stopped abruptly when I saw a woman at the counter purchase some candy. "Rio, you know I got a beef to pick with you right?"

He sighed, "Oh lord, what I do now? I know this ain't about that baby shower I gave you last week, 'Cause I didn't invite London, Ma did. Besides, everyone thought it was the bomb! "

"No, no that was fabulous. This ain't about that," I nodded thankfully. "We got beef because you didn't tell me about this new drug Orlando's been working on. You should have told me about that a long time ago."

Rio looked like he was caught in thought before he answered me. "I've only known about it for about two weeks. And I didn't tell you because I was sworn to secrecy until O ran all his tests and was ready to bring it to market."

"You've known about this for two weeks! And you didn't tell me!" Now I was genuinely pissed. "I don't give a damn if you were sworn to secrecy by Bishop TK

Wilson himself, that don't mean me; that means other people not me. You're not supposed to shut me out."

"Look I know this seems hard for you to comprehend, but I'm trying to build a relationship with my older brothers. I want them to trust me, Paris. Pop ain't gonna be around forever. I want them to know that we're a team and they can count on me."

"I hear you," despite his explanation I was still annoyed. "but you still wrong for that Rio. You know I wouldn't tell anybody. We're twins there isn't supposed to be any secrets between us, dammit. I tell you everything."

He stopped himself from taking another bite. "Don't even go there, cause you don't tell me everything." Believe it or not he had a little attitude himself.

"Yes, I do and you know it. What haven't I told you?" I eagerly challenged taking another bite of my sandwich.

"Oh yeah, you never told me who your baby daddy is, have you?" Not this shit again. I couldn't even finish chewing my food. He was sitting across the table, but it felt like he was all up in my face. "Why won't you tell me if it's Miguel or Trevor, huh?" he demanded.

I threw my sandwich back on the plate. "Because it's none of your fucking business, that's why, Rio! How many times I gotta tell you that?"

Rio threw his hands in the air. "See, that's what I'm talking about. You don't tell me everything. You tell me what you want me to know."

"What the hell does it matter which one it was? My baby ain't got no father anyway because both of them are dead. So I'd appreciate it if you stop asking me that shit." Disgusted by the whole conversation I stood up.

"Where are you going?" Rio asked.

"Upstairs to see if this heifer London had her baby yet. I guess your forgot, she's the one with the real baby daddy issues."

I left Rio with an attitude and headed back to the waiting area of the maternity ward where I was surprisingly greeted by a roomful of grim faces. When Rio and I left for the restaurant most of our family was leaning against each other trying to catch a nap until the doctor, or Harris came out the delivery room to tell us London's baby was born. There was no sign of the doctor but Harris was there sitting between my mother and father. His face was so scrunched up it looked like he was in pain. My parents' faces weren't doing much better. From the looks of it someone had just delivered some bad news and I knew exactly what it had to be.

"Oh shit! Don't tell me London's baby got straight hair and blue eyes?" There was a collective gasp from everyone in the room. Harris lifted his head and was the first to turn towards me. His face was crimson and his eyes were sending daggers of hate directly through me, but his look was nothing in comparison to the look my parents were giving me, especially my momma. I don't know what hell everyone was being all sensitive about anyway? We'd all known there was the possibility that London's baby might not be Harris. I mean it wasn't as if I was a secret that she was fucking that white boy Tony Dash around the same time the baby was conceived.

"She hasn't had the baby yet," Harris growled at me.

"Ooops, my bad," I replied then quickly changed the subject. "So why aren't you in the delivery room with my sister?" I asked Harris.

London and I had our issues, but she was still my sister. She was having my niece or nephew and with all these gloom and doom faces, I was actually worried there for a second. Although I would have liked to keep that bit of information to myself. "What's going on?"

"She's having some complications, so they asked me to wait out here," Harris replied.

"They're going to give her a C-section," my mother added.

"A C-section! Jesus Christ, I hope they don't do that to me." I ran my hand across my belly. "Last thing I want them doctors to do is cut me up so I'll have a scar. I plan on wearing a bikini to the beach this summer."

"Always about you isn't it, Paris?" Orlando laughed pathetically from cross the room.

I stuck up my middle finger. "Fuck you, Orlando! You just mad cause momma shot you down in the board meeting tonight."

"Paris," my father snapped before Orlando could reply, "sit your ass down and shut up!"

"He started it, Daddy," I said pointing at Orlando.

"And I'm ending it!" he demand with finality eying me the entire time, "Now sit your ass down. And shut up. Don't make me get out this chair and embarrass you. Do you hear me?"

The look he shot my way told me exactly what he had in mind and I did not want to get smacked in front of my entire family in a hospital. So, instead of lashing out and arguing, I plopped down in the seat. There weren't many people who could shut me up and get away with it. My father happened to be one of those people. Usually I could just bat my eyes at him and give him a puppy dog look and all would be forgive me, but that hadn't been working to well since I'd become pregnant.

"Yes, sir," I said humbly, but for me that was easier said than done because a sudden pain hit my stomach causing me to wince and instinctively place my hand over my belly. "Shitttt!"

"You okay?" Junior took me by the elbow guiding me towards a seat.

I took a breath holding onto the arm of the chair. "I'm okay the baby just kicked me like a mule, though. She's probably hungry. I should have finished eating that sandwich with Rio."

"You should have gone home like we told you. Lord knows you shouldn't be having no baby." My mother shook her head as she walked across the room towards me. "You can barely take care of yourself. How in heaven you gonna take care of a child."

"Momma," I fumed.

"Don't get upset with her," my father sighed. "Everything she said is the God damn truth. You don't need no baby, you're a damn baby yourself."

"Daddy!"

"Don't you Daddy me. How the hell could you be so irresponsible? I thought we raised you better than this."

"You did. I'm gonna be a good mother."

"I guess we'll see about that won't we," he sighed. "I know one thing. Your partying days are over."

After my father's verbal smack down a tense silence fell over my family. No one dared say anything to ignite another tongue-lashing. It was taking all my strength not to start wilding. My stomach was really rumbling and I wanted to kill my baby for making me feel this way.

Twenty minutes later a nurse entered the room and shouted, "Mr. Grant? Harris Grant?"

Harris slightly raised his hand as an acknowledgement. "That's me."

The nurse paused, "Would you like to come and meet your daughter?" She smiled wide.

Harris looked up at me and hesitantly said, "Uh-huh, I wanna see her."

"Congratulations brother-in-law," Orlando got up from his seat and patted Harris on the back breaking the room's uneasy tension and starting a round of congratulatory hugs and well wishing. For the next three or four minutes we were all one big happy family, but as Harris exited the room Daddy, Orlando and Junior gave each other a look. I knew exactly what they were thinking. I think the whole family was thinking the same thing: *I hope that baby comes out with nappy hair.*

"You want me to go in with him, Pop?" Junior asked my father. Junior was volunteering to go in there to make sure Harris didn't whip London's ass if the baby wasn't his. I wanted to go in there to watch him whip her ass.

"I'll go with him," I cut in.

My father shook his head. "No, he's not that stupid. I'm sure he's prepared for the worst, because if he does something stupid, I am." I looked at my family and instead of joy and relief there was still a look of anxiety on all of their faces.

"Oh shit." I said as the baby kicked.

"Paris, do not start. Now is not the time." My father warned.

"Oh shit!" I had a pretty high threshold for pain but this baby was kicking the shit out of me. "I'm not starting, Daddy."

"Yes, you are," He said in a low growl.

"No, I'm not." I doubled over. All of a sudden my stomach was now doing flips.

"Is she alright?" My sudden move caught the nosey nurse's attention. She came over and put her hand on my belly. I wanted to slap her hand away, but my stomach was taking all my attention.

"There's no need to be touching me. My baby's just kicking is all." I winced at the huge surge of pain in my stomach. It hurt so bad it felt like I was being split wide open.

"Honey, you've got a little more than a baby kicking going on there. Your water just broke. You're about to have your baby." The nurse pointed at the water dripping from the chair I was sitting in.

# Notes

# Notes

# Notes

## ORDER FORM
## URBAN BOOKS, LLC
78 E. Industry Ct
Deer Park, NY 11729

Name: (please print): _____

Address: _____

City/State: _____

Zip: _____

| QTY | TITLES | PRICE |
|---|---|---|
| | 16 On The Block | $14.95 |
| | A Girl From Flint | $14.95 |
| | A Pimp's Life | $14.95 |
| | Baltimore Chronicles | $14.95 |
| | Baltimore Chronicles 2 | $14.95 |
| | Betrayal | $14.95 |
| | Black Diamond | $14.95 |
| | Black Diamond 2 | $14.95 |
| | Black Friday | $14.95 |
| | Both Sides Of The Fence | $14.95 |
| | Both Sides Of The Fence 2 | $14.95 |
| | California Connection | $14.95 |

Shipping and handling-add $3.50 for 1st book, then $1.75 for each additional book.

Please send a check payable to:

**Urban Books, LLC**

Please allow 4-6 weeks for delivery

## ORDER FORM
## URBAN BOOKS, LLC
78 E. Industry Ct
Deer Park, NY 11729

Name: (please print):_____

Address:        _____

City/State:      _____

Zip:            _____

| QTY | TITLES | PRICE |
|-----|--------|-------|
|  | California Connection 2 | $14.95 |
|  | Cheesecake And Teardrops | $14.95 |
|  | Congratulations | $14.95 |
|  | Crazy In Love | $14.95 |
|  | Cyber Case | $14.95 |
|  | Denim Diaries | $14.95 |
|  | Diary Of A Mad First Lady | $14.95 |
|  | Diary Of A Stalker | $14.95 |
|  | Diary Of A Street Diva | $14.95 |
|  | Diary Of A Young Girl | $14.95 |
|  | Dirty Money | $14.95 |
|  | Dirty To The Grave | $14.95 |

Shipping and handling-add $3.50 for 1st book, then $1.75 for each additional book.
Please send a check payable to:
**Urban Books, LLC**
Please allow 4-6 weeks for delivery

# ORDER FORM
## URBAN BOOKS, LLC
### 78 E. Industry Ct
### Deer Park, NY 11729

Name: (please print): _____

Address: _____

City/State: _____

Zip: _____

| QTY | TITLES | PRICE |
|---|---|---|
| | Loving Dasia | $14.95 |
| | Material Girl | $14.95 |
| | Moth To A Flame | $14.95 |
| | Mr. High Maintenance | $14.95 |
| | My Little Secret | $14.95 |
| | Naughty | $14.95 |
| | Naughty 2 | $14.95 |
| | Naughty 3 | $14.95 |
| | Queen Bee | $14.95 |
| | Say It Ain't So | $14.95 |
| | Snapped | $14.95 |
| | Snow White | $14.95 |

Shipping and handling-add $3.50 for 1st book, then $1.75 for each additional book.

Please send a check payable to:

**Urban Books, LLC**

Please allow 4-6 weeks for delivery

5-13

## ORDER FORM
## URBAN BOOKS, LLC
78 E. Industry Ct
Deer Park, NY 11729

Name:(please print):_____

Address: _____

City/State: _____

Zip: _____

| QTY | TITLES | PRICE |
|-----|--------|-------|
| | Spoil Rotten | $14.95 |
| | Supreme Clientele | $14.95 |
| | The Cartel | $14.95 |
| | The Cartel 2 | $14.95 |
| | The Cartel 3 | $14.95 |
| | The Dopefiend | $14.95 |
| | The Dopeman Wife | $14.95 |
| | The Prada Plan | $14.95 |
| | The Prada Plan 2 | $14.95 |
| | Where There Is Smoke | $14.95 |
| | Where There Is Smoke 2 | $14.95 |
| | | |

Shipping and handling-add $3.50 for 1st book, then $1.75 for each additional book.

Please send a check payable to:

**Urban Books, LLC**

Please allow 4-6 weeks for delivery